T0329394

Gayle Sat Straight Up in Bed, Shaking Uncontrollably . . .

What had woken her—the dream? Or something else?

Slowly she pushed back the sheet and crept out of bed. She was burning up. She felt as if she was going to be sick, and she stumbled to the window to get some air.

Through a fog, she remembered her dream.

The fear and the panic.

The scratching of her nails against the lid of a coffin.

She opened the curtains and fumbled for the latch.

Bleary-eyed, she peered out into the night, out into the gnarled limbs of the maple tree.

And at first she thought it was a squirrel . . . a raccoon maybe . . . something with a long furry tail that was caught on the branch right outside the screen.

She saw her hands, in slow motion, raising the window.

And somehow she knew—even before she reached out—even before she caught the long, red tail-thing between her trembling fingers . . .

It wasn't a tail at all.

It was human hair.

Books by Richie Tankersley Cusick

BUFFY THE VAMPIRE SLAYER
(a novelization based on a screenplay by Joss Whedon)
THE DRIFTER
FATAL SECRETS
HELP WANTED
THE LOCKER
THE MALL
OVERDUE
SILENT STALKER
SOMEONE AT THE DOOR
SUMMER OF SECRETS
VAMPIRE

Available from ARCHWAY Paperbacks

RICHIE TANKERSLEY
CUSICK

Summer of Secrets

AN ARCHWAY PAPERBACK
Published by POCKET BOOKS
New York London Toronto Sydney Tokyo Singapore

AN ARCHWAY PAPERBACK *Original*

An Archway Paperback published by
POCKET BOOKS, a division of Simon & Schuster Inc.
1230 Avenue of the Americas, New York, NY 10020

ISBN: 978-1-4814-0160-9

First Archway Paperback printing July 1996

10 9 8 7 6 5 4 3 2 1

AN ARCHWAY PAPERBACK and colophon are registered trademarks of Simon & Schuster Inc.

Cover art by Bill Schmidt

Printed in the U.S.A.

IL 7+

To Stephanie
for loving me through my worst adventure

Summer of Secrets

"No malls," Stephanie grumbled.

"What?" On the front seat beside her, Gayle Nelson roused from a fitful doze, just managing to catch the road map before it slid from her knees onto the floor.

"I said, no malls," Stephanie Borders repeated solemnly. "No malls, no movies—no McDonald's, either, probably." She clutched the steering wheel with one hand, using the other to motion toward the windshield. "Just look out there! All I've seen for the last fifty miles are cornfields and cows! Oh—and one tractor!" She gave a pathetic moan, her eyes widening dramatically, as only Stephanie's could do. "We're gonna be stuck out here for two whole weeks!"

"You make it sound like some sort of death sentence," Gayle chided. "Smell that country air! Those flowers! Those apple trees we just passed!"

Stephanie's voice rose plaintively. "What apple trees? I can't smell anything but manure!"

"Oh, stop it. Think about when we get to Aunt Pat's. The homemade chocolate chip cookies and fresh lemonade. And a big juicy watermelon in the refrigerator. And don't forget my very favorite— sausage quiche."

"Sausage quiche? Isn't that a little—you know— *gourmet* for farm people?"

Gayle ignored the sarcasm. "Nobody makes it like Aunt Pat. In fact, she's won lots of blue ribbons for that quiche at county fairs."

"Wow. I'm so impressed."

"Will you stop? You'll really love her, Steph. She's such a character—my favorite person in the whole world."

"More favorite than me?"

"Well . . . different from you. My favorite *old* person in the whole world."

"And you're her favorite niece."

"I guess I am. Though I'm not supposed to be spreading that around to the rest of the family."

"Like they haven't figured it out by now? I don't see them being invited up here."

"They hate the country, and they're nothing at all like her. Aunt Pat's a free spirit. She's fun and . . . exciting."

"She raises chickens." Stephanie's eyebrow arched. "How fun and exciting can someone be who raises chickens?"

"She *used* to raise chickens," Gayle pointed out, amused. "And cows." Then thinking a moment, she added, "But since she fell and broke her hip last year, I'm not sure how much she does around the farm anymore. That's the *first* reason Mom and

Dad wanted me to come. They want to know how she's really doing."

"But you said she always sounds great on the phone."

"She *does* sound great. That doesn't mean she *is* great. This way I can see for myself."

"So what's the *second* reason they wanted you to come?" Stephanie asked dryly.

"She's selling off part of her farm." Gayle sighed and shook her head. "God, I hate to see her do that. It breaks my heart."

"So tell her not to."

"I wish I could. But some developers offered her a ton of money to sell off some of the acreage, and she thinks it's the sensible thing to do. She wants to put the money away—says it'll come in handy when Dad has to put her in a nursing home."

Stephanie looked impressed. "She sounds pretty smart to me."

"I guess so. It's just weird, knowing this is the last time I'll see the farm the way it's always been. I have this feeling about developers, see? I think they'll keep asking her for more and more land, and pretty soon there won't be anything left at all."

"I think that's called progress."

"I hate progress."

Stephanie chuckled. "So when was the last time you were here?"

"Three summers ago." Gayle smiled softly. "I used to come practically every summer to see her. Then . . . I don't know . . . I started getting busy, I guess." She pushed back her hair and gently touched one earlobe. "These earrings I always wear? Aunt Pat gave them to me years ago. They make me feel closer to her somehow."

Stephanie shrugged. "Things happen like that, people drifting apart. My whole family used to spend summers at the beach—then we all started growing up and doing different things. Now we hardly see each other till school starts again. Frankly, I think my folks enjoy it. I don't think they miss us at all."

"Steph, watch out—don't hit that turtle."

"What turtle?" Stephanie demanded. Peering out the windshield, she managed to swerve the car just in time.

"Remember—critters have the right of way around here," Gayle reminded her with a laugh, but Stephanie only groaned.

"Why did I ever let you talk me into this?"

"'Cause you're my best friend, and you'd do anything in the world for me?"

Stephanie's look was lethal.

"'Cause being on vacation with me was better than going with your parents?" Gayle tried again. "And having to visit your sister with the bratty kids?"

"You got it." Stephanie sighed. "But I wish you'd told your aunt I was coming with you."

"I tried. I called four different times yesterday, but I never could get her. Relax—she'll be thrilled you came along."

"I hope so. I feel rude just dropping in like this."

"It was a last-minute decision—no big deal. And cheer up. I know for a fact that Pine Ridge has *two* movie theaters. And one whole street full of junk food."

4

Stephanie gave a grudging nod. "But you said your aunt doesn't live in town."

"She doesn't. But ten miles *from* town isn't exactly a foreign country."

"Could've fooled me."

Gayle hid a smile and peered out her window into the gathering dusk. The sun was barely visible now over the distant hills. The rolling fields and wooded valleys that had stretched endlessly around them all afternoon were fast disappearing behind a curtain of twilight, and the narrow road wound off into shadows. Two weeks in the country, Gayle reminded herself—two weeks without her parents griping or her two younger brothers hanging around, two weeks without household chores or being told what to do and when to do it . . . just two wonderful weeks of peace and quiet and Aunt Pat's hospitality.

"No guys," Stephanie mumbled. "No dates . . . no passionate summer romances . . ."

"Oh, like you'd have so many at home," Gayle threw back at her. They two of them had been best friends since middle school, and the ongoing joke was that neither of them had ever found "Mr. Right." Not that Stephanie couldn't have her pick of anyone in the world, Gayle thought somewhat enviously, glancing over at Steph's long black hair and green eyes and perfect figure with its perfect tan. On the contrary, Gayle had grown up always being the tallest in her class and was prone to freckles when she stayed in the sun too long.

"Is that my fault?" Stephanie's indignant tone brought Gayle back again. "I happen to be very selective about who I date."

"Selective how?"

"They *must* be alive and breathing. It's an absolute requirement of mine."

"You're asking a lot," Gayle said, straight-faced. "No wonder you never go out."

The two of them exchanged looks, then burst out laughing.

"Well, it's not like we're ugly or anything," Stephanie tried to point out between giggles.

"Really? I hadn't noticed."

"I mean, take you, for instance. You have *great* hair."

"That's it? Great hair? Wow . . . I guess I have a lot going for me, huh?"

"Nobody in school has great red hair like yours."

"And it's not even from a bottle."

"Guys *love* red hair."

"So if my whole body was covered with it, then maybe I'd have a boyfriend?"

Stephanie ignored her. "And I've got . . ." she frowned, then blurted out, "refined features!"

"Hmmm . . ."

"You know. Like royalty. My family *is* descended from French aristocracy, you know."

"Whatever you say."

"And you're very smart. And I'm very witty. It's a winning combination, and I really think—"

"That neither of us has any sense of direction, or we'd be at Aunt Pat's by now," Gayle broke in.

"You're right. You said ten miles outside of town, and we drove through Pine Ridge at least twenty minutes ago."

Gayle stared at the map, then tossed it on the

floor. "I can't make any sense of this thing. Maybe we missed our turn."

"Maybe? Don't you know? *How* many times have you been here?"

"Well, Dad always drove. And you know I never pay attention when someone else is driving—"

"So what were you gonna do? Just let me keep going till we ended up in the next state? We've been on the road for nearly twelve hours! What's a couple more!"

"Okay, you've made your point. Turn around."

"And where do you suggest I do that?" Stephanie squinted and leaned over the steering wheel. "This isn't exactly a two-lane road, in case you hadn't noticed. In fact, I think I'm being *very* generous calling it a lane and a half."

"Then keep going till you see a place wide enough."

"That could take days."

"Stephanie, what are you doing?"

"I'm backing up."

"You can't do that!"

"No? Just watch me."

"You'll wreck my car!"

"Well, you shouldn't have asked me to drive."

"Steph!"

Gayle felt the gears shift and the sudden burst of backward speed. As she started to turn in her seat, there was a squealing of tires, and then a loud crash as the car slammed to a halt.

Stunned, she gazed over at Stephanie, who was looking back at her in total disbelief.

"In case you hadn't noticed," Gayle said dryly,

"we're not moving." She rolled down her window and peered out. "Probably cause we're stuck to the pickup truck right behind us."

"What do you mean, truck?" Stephanie's voice rose angrily. "I didn't see any truck!"

Without warning a fist banged against Stephanie's window, and both girls screamed.

"Lock your door!" Gayle cried, rolling her window up again. Then she grabbed her friend as a tall figure leaned down to peer at them through the glass.

Two clenched hands lowered to the side of the car. As the stranger's face appeared in the window, Gayle could see his chiseled face, his tight cheekbones and firmly set jaw. Dark narrowed eyes glared in at them, and dark wavy hair hung loosely to his shoulders, framing both sides of his deeply tanned face.

For an endless moment all Gayle could do was stare. She heard his fist pound again on the glass. She heard the unmistakable sound of Stephanie opening the window.

"You jerk!" Stephanie railed at him. "Where're your lights! Don't you people use headlights around here?"

The young man's eyes shifted toward the far horizon, to the last feeble rays of sun glowing over the hills. Burnished shadows played sharply over the angles of his face, and his glance slid smoothly from Stephanie to Gayle and then back again.

"Don't people drive forward where you come from?" he said at last. His voice was deep and very calm. Gayle couldn't tell if he was teasing or getting ready to explode.

8

"Well"—Gayle made an attempt at humor—"we do when we know where we're going."

The stranger didn't answer. His expression didn't change.

Gayle tried again. "I have insurance, okay? It was our fault, and we're sorry. We'll pay for any damage."

At last the young man shrugged his shoulders. "You're the one with damage. You didn't hurt my truck."

"So glad to hear it," Stephanie muttered. She leaned back into the seat and pressed both hands to her forehead. "Isn't this wonderful. A vacation to die for."

The stranger's gaze never wavered. Gayle tried to read his impenetrable stare, and felt a slow chill work up her spine.

"Hope you're not going far," he said at last.

"You couldn't possibly hope it as much as I do," Stephanie retorted, but Gayle moved closer, her voice anxious.

"What do you mean? Is our car hurt that bad?"

"I mean," he said, taking a step back, "I feel sorry for whoever's on the road with you."

"Excuse us, won't you." Stephanie shot him an icy smile. "We have places to go and civilized people to see."

"No, not yet." Gayle turned her door handle and started to climb out. "I want to look at the car—"

"You can look at it later."

"No, Steph, wait!"

Hearing the rev of the engine, she just managed to pull inside and slam the door again as Stephanie floored the accelerator.

"Later, farm boy!" Stephanie yelled. With a flurry of gravel she shot back onto the road, then cast Gayle a surly glance. "What? What's wrong?"

"Are you crazy!" Gayle burst out. "Driving like a maniac! Calling that guy names! If we don't end up dying in a wreck, he'll probably come after us and kill us himself! I can't believe you did that! And we're still going the wrong way!"

"I told you, there's no place to turn around—uh-oh, the trunk just flew up—"

"Stop the car!"

"But what if he's following us? *You're* the one who said he might follow us—"

"Do you want all our stuff to fall out? Look, there's a place up there—pull off!"

Obediently Stephanie began to slow down. "It looks like a fruit stand," she said, easing the car toward the side of the road. "I don't think it's open, though—"

"Shut up, and stop the car."

Grumbling, Stephanie pulled off onto the wide shoulder. Immediately a cloud of dust enveloped the car, and as they waited for it to settle, they saw the pickup truck pass them and disappear down the road.

"Still no headlights," Stephanie observed, but Gayle ignored her and began rummaging through the glove box for a flashlight.

"He really is a menace to society," Stephanie insisted. She thought a minute, then added, "Such as it is out here."

Gayle sighed loudly and shoved open her door. "Are you coming or not?"

"Sure."

Together they got out and went around to the back of the car. The rear bumper was smashed, and both taillights were shattered. Gayle stood silently, surveying the crumpled lid of the trunk, all too aware of the darkness thickening around them.

"Let's just hope nobody gets behind us on the road," she said with a sigh.

"Yeah, like a cop or something. I'd hate to get a ticket in a place like this. Or do they just arrest you and throw you in with perverts?"

"Stephanie, don't talk to me." Abruptly Gayle walked off, leaving her friend to stare after her.

"Maybe we can find something to tie the trunk with," Stephanie suggested, running a little to catch up.

"Why don't you just get *inside* the trunk and *hold* it shut?"

"Oh, come on, it's not that bad."

"Just start putting our stuff in the backseat, okay? I'm going to look for some rope."

As Stephanie gave a sullen nod and turned her attention to the car, Gayle walked over to the roadside stand. Funny how something so normal could look so creepy now, she thought, playing her flashlight over the lopsided structure of warped, rotted boards. Weeds grew knee-high around it. Broken crates littered the ground, and trash had blown up against a line of straggly elms, tangled in piles of dead leaves and brambles. Not a single car passed now on the road. There wasn't a breath of wind.

"You're not gonna find anything out here," Stephanie called impatiently. "Let's just go."

"We can't drive with the trunk like that. There

must be a piece of rope or string or something we can use."

"Will you please be careful? There are probably snakes out here."

Gayle paused, shining her flashlight out ahead of her. Her gaze swept over some empty crates . . . piles of old wood and splintered lumber . . . clumps of litter and dead leaves . . .

"See anything?" Stephanie yelled.

"No." Gayle took a cautious step, then hesitated once again. The air smelled of dust and heat and overripe fruit. *And something bad,* she realized with a start.

"Come on, Gayle, this place is creepy!"

Something bad, Gayle thought again, but she didn't know why she'd thought that, nor could she actually identify the smell. *Something bad . . . something . . .*

Dead?

"I can't fit any more in the backseat!" Stephanie shouted.

"Then wait for me in the car!"

"Look, just bring the flashlight over here, and I'll go through my suitcase. We can tie the trunk with a sock or something and—Gayle!"

But Gayle was moving farther away, eyes intent on the ground, flashlight steady in front of her. "Here's a path, Steph! I wonder where it goes?"

"Nowhere!" her friend answered firmly. "Now, come *on!*"

Oblivious to Stephanie's protests, Gayle kept on for several yards, following the narrow pathway through the weeds. She could hear Stephanie coming behind her now, stomping through the underbrush and swearing loudly.

"Gayle, I've got stickers all over me and they're—ouch! Will you stop?"

But Gayle had already stopped, and as Stephanie ran into her, Gayle steadied her friend and aimed the flashlight off to their left. Here the ground sloped downward, forming a broad shallow ravine that was heaped with garbage and odds and ends of blackened debris.

"Look, Steph, someone's been burning trash. There's got to be a rope in a trash pile, right?"

"I don't know, and I don't care. I mean it—I'm leaving without you!"

"Oh, Steph, don't be such a baby. Wait for me."

"What are you doing?"

But Gayle was already clambering down the slope, her flashlight held protectively in front of her. As she reached the bottom, she perched at the edge and slowly ran the thin beam of light over the contents of the dump. A can dislodged and fell, startling her, and as Stephanie let out a squeal, Gayle saw the dark shape of a rat scurry out of sight beneath one end of a filthy, half-burnt mattress.

"That does it!" Stephanie exclaimed angrily. "That's it, Gayle. I'm really going this time!"

"Wait—look! I found something!"

Before Stephanie could answer, Gayle slid down several more feet, stabbing her flashlight at the mattress. A frayed length of rope was showing beneath one end, and as Gayle took hold of it and began to pull, she glanced back at Stephanie with a frown.

"Come and help me!"

"No way. No way are you gonna get me down there."

"Then at least hold the flashlight while I do this."

Stephanie shook her head. Biting back a nasty reply, Gayle tugged harder on the rope, then straightened in surprise.

"What is it?" Stephanie asked suspiciously.

"I'm not sure. Looks like a bag."

"A what?"

"You know, like a laundry bag or something."

"Leave it alone, and come on."

"The rope must be part of the drawstring. Maybe I can pull it loose."

"Well, for God's sake, be careful."

"It's wedged under this stupid mattress." Gayle frowned and tugged harder. *Something bad . . . something dead . . .* She glanced nervously from side to side but couldn't see anything unusual. She worked with clumsy fingers at the mouth of the bag, trying to loosen it, trying to pull the rope free.

"Come *on!*" Stephanie moaned.

"Okay, okay, I've almost got it."

She saw Stephanie make a face, then turn away and start back to the car. She felt her own fingers working into the bag and the material stretching in her hands. The bag was opening now—she was almost certain she could get the rope out if she tore it. Clenching her teeth, she made a huge rip in the top of the bag.

And then she froze.

"Bye, Gayle!" Stephanie shouted angrily. "I'll see you back at the car!"

"Steph . . ." and suddenly Gayle's voice sounded strange, so strange and so distant, like someone else's voice, and her body was locked in place, and she couldn't move, all she could do was stare. . . .

"What's wrong?" she heard Stephanie call, and again her own voice came out, faint and trembling and full of horror. . . .

"I . . . found something," Gayle whispered.

"Let me guess—an old hamburger. Come on, Gayle, I'm *starving!*"

"Steph . . . Stephanie . . ."

"What? What's wrong?"

And she could hear the sudden fear in Stephanie's voice, but not as icy cold as the fear in her own voice, as the fear in her own heart, as she stared and stared at the thing poking out of the bag, lying there at her feet. . . .

"No . . ." Gayle murmured, "I'm not okay. . . ."

And Stephanie running, sliding down the incline toward her, Stephanie's fingers digging into her shoulder, forcing her around—

"Gayle? What *is* it!"

And somehow she managed to turn back again, managed to aim her flashlight so Stephanie could see for herself. . . .

"Oh, God . . . it's an arm."

2

Darkness rushed at them from all sides.

For a moment Gayle thought she might actually pass out, but she forced herself to take a deep breath and tried to concentrate on the thin beam of flashlight as it wavered off through the shadows. She felt Stephanie's grip close around hers, firmly guiding the flashlight back again to the horrible sight on the ground.

"Only part of an arm." Stephanie's voice was barely a whisper. "And look at it—"

But Gayle had already gotten as good a look as she wanted. Most of it had been burnt beyond recognition, but part of the hand and wrist were still visible beneath a black layer of blisters.

"Is it real?" Stephanie mumbled. "Maybe it's not real, maybe it's a fake arm, you know, like one of those things you can buy at Halloween. . . ."

But as Stephanie kept the flashlight focused, Gayle could see the awful thing lying there, fleshless fingers pointed straight at them, and somehow she knew better.

"It's real," Gayle said softly. "Steph . . . who could have done this?"

Stephanie shook her head. "Do you think the rest of it's in that bag?"

She cautiously prodded the bag with her shoe. Gayle gasped and pulled her back.

"What are you *doing!*"

"Well, I'm not going to *open* the bag! Can't you pull the top a little more and—what's wrong?"

"Are you crazy! Leave it alone—it's *horrible!*"

"But there's probably a body in there! Don't you want to see who it is? What if it's not dead?"

The possibility was too horrifying to even consider. Gayle tugged on Stephanie's hand, trying to drag her away.

"I want to go. I want to go now."

"Wait a minute!" Jerking free, Stephanie took a step closer. "Look—don't you see that?"

"See what?"

Stephanie grabbed the flashlight, aiming it down onto the charred fingers.

"It looks like a ring. There—can't you see it?"

"I don't want to see it," Gayle insisted. "I want to go!"

"But it might be a clue or something! Can we get it off?"

"Oh, my God . . ."

Undaunted, Stephanie nudged the fingers again with the toe of her shoe. Then she bent closer, studying it beneath the glare of the flashlight.

"I can't make it out, it's all black. But I think it

might be a flower on the ring. Can you see it—does it look like a rose or some kind of flower?"

But Gayle was shaking her head wildly, reaching out to clutch her friend's arm. "Ssh!"

"What?"

Gayle's voice went tight. "Do you hear something?"

"What kind of—"

"Footsteps. Over there!"

"Where? I don't—"

"Listen!"

Without warning a light burst on, pinning them where they stood, blinding them from the opposite side of the dump. Instinctively Gayle's hands went up to shield herself from the glare, and the flashlight thudded to the ground. Stephanie let out a surprised cry, but Gayle couldn't see her, couldn't see anything at all. The light was so intense that all she could do was stand there helplessly with her hands over her eyes.

"Who's there!" She heard the fear in Stephanie's voice. "What do you want?"

There was no answer. The shadows were absolutely still. And then, just as quickly as it had appeared, the light went out, plunging them into darkness.

For several heart-stopping seconds Gayle could only stand there blinking, trying to adjust again to the gloom. She felt Stephanie trip and stumble beside her, and she groped out for her friend's arm.

"Steph, are you all right?"

"Where's the flashlight—I can't find the flashlight—"

"Forget the flashlight—let's get out of here!"

Together they scrambled out of the dump and raced back to the car. With their broken trunk forgotten now, all they could think of was getting away, and within minutes they were heading back toward town.

For a long while neither of them spoke. It was Stephanie who finally broke the silence.

"I bet I know what that light was," she said, yet Gayle could hear the false confidence in her voice. "One of those spotlights with a motion sensor. I bet we walked too close to it, and the stupid thing came on."

Slowly Gayle shook her head. "I don't think so. A security light would've been up higher, wouldn't it?" When Stephanie didn't answer, she added, "I think it was someone with a really strong flashlight. Remember, I heard footsteps just before."

"You *thought* you heard footsteps."

Gayle considered this and forced a nervous laugh. "Listen to us. It was probably just someone out walking in the woods. And he didn't expect to see us there. He was probably just as scared as we were."

"Then why didn't he say anything?"

That unsettling quiet filled the car again. Gayle's hands tightened on the wheel.

"Maybe whoever owns the property heard us and came to see what was going on," she said. "Maybe we were trespassing, and they were trying to scare us off."

Stephanie shifted in her seat, casting Gayle a sidelong glance. "It was a roadside stand. How could we be trespassing at a roadside stand?"

"I don't know," Gayle said miserably. "But that

path might have led somewhere if we'd kept on it. There could have been a house back there, right? Someone might have lived there, right?"

"With an arm in their garbage dump?"

"Oh, God," Gayle whispered, "I wish we hadn't left it back there."

"What *should* we have done—brought it with us? Oh, nice to see you, too, Aunt Pat, and here's a little hostess gift we thought you'd enjoy—"

"It's not funny! You're right—we should've at least looked in that bag. We've got to tell someone. We've got to tell the police."

"Now? Two girls who don't even live here going in and saying they found a burnt arm in a garbage dump? Do you think they'll believe us?"

"I don't know. Okay, let's tell Aunt Pat and have *her* tell the police."

Stephanie was calmer now, and some of the old humor crept back into her voice. "This could only happen to us. You realize that, don't you?"

"And you were afraid Pine Ridge would be boring—I hope you're satisfied." Gayle eased up on the gas pedal and pointed to the windshield. "I think this might be our turn."

"How can you tell with all those trees hanging down? It's so dark out here."

"Yeah, I noticed that," Gayle said uneasily. "It never looks this dark at home."

Slowing the car, she eased it onto a side road, then braced herself as the tires sank at once into deep holes. The road wasn't paved—as they crept along, rocking from side to side, dust spewed up into the headlights, making it almost impossible to see. Tree limbs clawed at the sides of the car and scraped along the roof. From time to time a glimpse of moonlight filtered down through the leaves, transforming the dust to a silvery haze.

"Can you see anything?" Stephanie asked nervously.

"No. But I think the road's getting narrower."

"Are you *sure* this is the right way?"

"Well . . . pretty sure."

"Why would anyone want to live way out here in the middle of nowhere?" Stephanie asked incredulously. "I'd be scared to death."

"I told you, Aunt Pat's a real character. And believe me, she's not scared of *anything.*" As Gayle maneuvered the car around a sharp curve, she gave a sigh of relief. "We're here, Steph. There's her mailbox."

"Where?"

"There. By the driveway."

"That's a driveway?" Stephanie gazed uncertainly at a gap between two fenceposts.

"And there's the house up there," Gayle said triumphantly. "At the top of the hill."

"You sure?"

"Of course I'm sure."

"Then how come everything's so dark?"

Gayle hesitated, her eyes following the direction of the headlights. She could see the dirt drive extending some thirty yards upward, to the tall familiar house standing loftily beneath its even taller trees. She could remember many summers when her family had pulled in here at nightfall— could remember the warm, welcoming glow greeting them from the wide front porch and every window, upstairs and down. . . .

21

But tonight was different.

Tonight the house was completely black.

Stephanie let out a groan. "You *did* tell her we'd be here today, didn't you?"

"Of course I told her." Gayle frowned.

"Maybe she didn't get the letter."

"I called her, Steph. I talked to her myself. Mom and I both talked to her. She was so excited—she couldn't wait for us to come."

Stephanie didn't answer.

"I'm sure it's fine," Gayle said confidently. "She probably got busy somewhere and just hasn't gotten home yet."

Still Stephanie said nothing. Gayle urged the car up the hill and pulled to a stop beside the house. She turned off the motor but left the headlights on, and together they sat there, staring out at the front steps, the front porch, the dark outline of the front door.

"Well," Gayle said finally, "the house is probably open. Most people out here still leave their doors unlocked."

She started to turn when Stephanie's hand clamped hard around her elbow.

"Don't go out there," Stephanie murmured. "Someone's watching us."

Gayle's blood froze in her veins.

She could see Stephanie gazing out into the darkness, could see Stephanie's mouth slightly opened, as though she wanted to scream but couldn't.

The old house rose before them, windows blank and gaping, like sockets in a skull. A thick tangle of ivy and shrubbery crawled along the front walls, overflowing both sides of the steps, climbing up the wooden railings and columns of the porch, and spilling down across the floorboards on the other side. There was a porch swing hanging at one end. Most of it was hidden in shadows, but as Stephanie pointed to it, Gayle could see the two eyes staring fiendishly back at them from the darkness.

"There!" Stephanie gasped. *"There!"*

Gayle couldn't move.

The eyes held her, paralyzed, and all she could do was stare back at them in terror.

And then, suddenly, she flung open her door and jumped out.

"Gayle, no!" Stephanie shouted. "What are you doing!"

"You idiot!" Gayle shouted back angrily, leaning into the car. "Don't you even recognize a cat when you see one?"

Stephanie looked blank. "A . . . cat?"

"A cat!" Gayle exploded. "I swear, Steph, one of these days—"

Leaving the threat unfinished, she marched up the steps and made a grab toward the swing. Immediately there was a hissing sound, and then a huge cat leaped down, flicking its tail in annoyance before stalking away.

"Well, how would I know?" Stephanie grumbled, climbing out of the car. "I've never had a pet in my life."

"Aunt Pat?" Gayle yelled. "We're here!" Feeling braver now, she went to the door and knocked. When there was no answer, she knocked again, stepping back in surprise as the door moved slightly beneath her hand.

"You're right," Stephanie said, coming up behind her. "Looks like it's open."

"Then she must be here. Somewhere."

Stephanie looked doubtful. "Maybe the power's out, and she fell asleep."

"She'd have heard your big mouth by now."

Together they went inside. While Stephanie waited near the door, Gayle found the lightswitch, and a second later the living room sprang to life around them. It was a cozy, comfortable room.

Flowered wallpaper, lace curtains, overstuffed furniture, fresh flowers in vases—everything was just as Gayle remembered, and she turned to Stephanie with a relieved smile.

"She probably just ran to the store or something," Gayle assured her. "Let's go ahead and bring our stuff in."

"How about *I* bring the stuff in—*you* find us something to eat. And put some lights on out here, will you?"

After several tries Gayle located the switch for the outdoor floodlights. Stephanie gave her a thumbs-up sign as she headed back to the car, and Gayle went at once to the kitchen. The smell of chocolate still lingered in the air, and she stood for a moment, gazing down at the neat rows of cookies laid out on the large pine tabletop. Pots and pans hung from the raftered ceiling, and odds and ends of crockery lined the shelves along one wall. Gayle picked up a cookie, bit into it, then put it back down. Strange . . . Aunt Pat's cookies were always soft and chewy—she never let them get hard like these.

"Aunt Pat?" she called.

There wasn't a sound in the house. Gayle stood listening a minute more, then decided to make a search of the other rooms on the first floor.

"I think this is all of it," Stephanie announced as Gayle walked into the living room. All their stuff was heaped in the middle of the floor, and Gayle shook her head, staring at the pile in dismay.

"Did we really bring all that for just two weeks?"

Stephanie flopped into a chair and shook the hair

back from her eyes. "Yes, we really did. You never know what you might need this far from civilization. Is it my imagination or is it hot in here?"

"I warned you about that, Steph. She doesn't have central air like you're used to, you know—this is an old house."

"You promised she'd have air-conditioning. I can't survive without air-conditioning."

"I told you she had window units. And you'll just have to make the best of it."

"Where are you going now?"

"To look upstairs."

"I'm telling you, your aunt's not here. She probably had second thoughts about us coming, and she left town. What matters most right now is that she left food in the refrigerator."

"Would you settle for cookies on the table?" Gayle pointed in the direction of the kitchen, and Stephanie promptly disappeared.

The second floor yielded no more clues than the first. Gayle wandered through the high-ceilinged bedrooms, the homey hodgepodge of antiques and folk art, turning on lights as she went. The farmhouse itself was over a century old, and with every visit Gayle had made here through the years, it seemed Aunt Pat had always found one more thing to lovingly restore. *Lovingly*—that was the perfect word, Gayle decided—for everything Aunt Pat touched became something beautiful.

"Hey, Gayle!"

Gayle stopped in the hallway to admire an old family photograph as Stephanie shouted from the kitchen. "What?"

"Did you see this note?"

"What note?"

"The one here on the counter by the coffeepot!"

Frowning, Gayle went back down. Stephanie had managed to devour nearly half a dozen of the cookies and was sitting at the table. As Gayle sat across from her, Stephanie thrust a sheet of paper into her hand.

"You were right," Stephanie said. "She must have gone to the store or something."

Gayle stared down at the note.

There were only three words printed there, in large penciled letters: BE BACK SOON.

Frowning, Gayle lowered the paper and stared at Stephanie.

"This is weird."

"It is?"

"Well, if she was coming back soon, she'd have left the lights on for us."

"Unless she left before it got dark."

"But the note says 'soon.' So why isn't she back by now?"

"You're driving me crazy, you know that?" Stephanie leaned forward, her eyebrows lifting in annoyance. "You're making something out of nothing. I mean, how many times have you and I gone shopping for *one* hour that turns into *six?*"

Gayle almost laughed at that. "You're right. It's just . . ."

"Just what?"

"I don't know. I guess it was finding that arm. We've *got* to tell someone, Steph."

"You said your aunt would know what to do, so

try and stop thinking about it," Stephanie ordered, then pointed to a doorway at the rear of the kitchen. "What's back there?"

"A porch." Automatically Gayle began walking toward it, her uneasiness growing. The porch was enclosed, with windows on three walls, and a screen door that opened onto a stoop in the side yard. Gayle looked out at the thick bushes clumped around the steps, at the large metal cans overflowing with trash. Moonlight shone brightly, illuminating the huge expanse of lawn, the thick foliage of trees, the dark shapes of the barn and the chicken house and various other outbuildings scattered back from the house.

"Aunt Pat!" she called.

An owl hooted mournfully from some distant treetop. Hills rose up on every side, closing them off from the world.

Gayle came back in and regarded Stephanie with a solemn frown. For a long moment Stephanie gazed back at her, then finally relented with a sigh.

"Okay. Do you know her neighbors?"

"No."

"You want to call your parents?"

"Of course not. They'd be worried sick. They'd be on their way up here before I could even get off the phone."

"My point exactly. Now where are you going?"

Rummaging through a kitchen drawer, Gayle pulled out a flashlight. Then she shoved open the screen and looked back at Stephanie. "Maybe she's out back . . . in the barn or something."

"Want me to come with you?"

"No. I won't be long."

The barn sat a few hundred yards away, downhill and to the west of the house, surrounded by a wooden fence that enclosed the spacious barnyard. In the silvery wash of moonlight nothing seemed to have aged since her childhood, and even before she reached it, Gayle could smell the hay and grain, the dust and manure, all mixed together with the dead, dry heat of a summer's night.

"Aunt Pat!"

The door creaked slowly on rusted hinges. To Gayle's surprise, a horse whinnied, stamping its feet at her intrusion. There was a flurry of wings from the rafters as birds startled uneasily in the overhead loft. Gayle felt for the lightswitch and worked it up and down, but nothing happened.

She stood there uncertainly, keeping one hand on the latch, sweeping the cavernous interior with her flashlight. The barn was thick with shadows. Dust motes swam in the pale beam of her light, giving everything a hazy, dreamlike quality, and as the birds fluttered once more above her head, she started at the sound. She could see the feedway through the center of the room, the open area to the left where Aunt Pat had kept cows many years ago, the two wooden stalls farther down, the mounds and mounds of loose straw across the packed earth floor to the right. She could hear the unmistakable sounds of mice burrowing beneath the hay and feed, and again the horse gave a restless murmur.

"Aunt Pat?" she called softly.

A cat mewed quietly from one far corner. At once Gayle aimed her flashlight and saw the half-open door of a storeroom and the cat that perched there on the step, its huge eyes calm and unafraid.

Slowly she swept her light up the walls and across the ceiling, lingering a moment on the hayloft. She could see the opening in the loft floor above, mounds of hay stuffed beyond it. The air was close and still, yet as she continued to stare at the loft, she could swear she heard a faint rustling sound. . . .

"Aunt Pat?" Gayle whispered. "Is anyone there?"

The shadows throbbed around her.

Several pieces of hay dribbled down from the opening . . . down onto the giant haystack below.

Gayle felt the hairs prickle along the back of her neck. Gripping the flashlight even tighter, she shone it at the haystack and began to move forward. Something brushed her shoulder and she gasped, realizing in the next instant that it was only a coil of rope hanging from one of the wooden posts. Bags of feed leaned against a section of one wall; tools hung from old, rusty nails. As Gayle neared the haystack, she paused and held her breath, listening. She couldn't hear a sound from the loft. Nothing fell from the opening now.

She started to turn back.

She started to turn back toward the door when something stopped her.

Another sound . . .

A *sharper* sound . . .

As though *another* foot had crunched down upon straw at the very same instant her own foot touched the floor.

Gayle could feel the flashlight digging into her palm. She forced herself to take a deep, deep breath.

Just a mouse, Gayle, that's all it is . . . get a grip, for God's sake . . . it's just a stupid mouse trying to get away from that stupid cat. . . .

Slowly Gayle's stomach began to tighten.

She put a hand to her head, and her heart began to pound.

Get out of here! Get out of here now!

In a burst of panic Gayle lunged forward. Stumbling outside, she managed to catch herself with both hands as she toppled over onto the grass.

She didn't dare look back.

Somehow she got to her feet again and raced wildly to the house.

 **4**

"You know how you are," Stephanie said for the fourth time. "You know how you imagine things."

"Right. Like I imagined that arm?"

Gayle slammed the kitchen door behind them, watching in frustration as Stephanie sat down calmly at the table.

"Okay, I'm sorry" Stephanie sighed. "I *didn't* hear anything in the barn. I didn't *feel* anything in the barn. It didn't scare me, Gayle—it was just a barn!"

Gayle shook her head. She ran a glass of water from the tap and took a long, slow sip. The glass trembled in her hand. "Something was there."

"Of course something was there. The horse was there. You didn't tell me she had a horse."

"I didn't *know* she had a horse. And anyway, it *wasn't* the horse. It was something else."

"Okay, fine. Something else. How do you know?"

"I know. It was something. Or someone."

"A rat? A snake?"

Again Gayle shook her head.

"Well . . ." Stephanie reached for another cookie. "Barns are infested with varmints, aren't they? Isn't that what animals are called out here—varmints?" When Gayle didn't laugh, she sighed and put her cookie back down. "Okay, fine, I'll humor you. Do you want to go out there one more time and look around?"

"No."

"Do you think whatever it was is still there?"

"I don't know. But maybe the horse felt it, too. Maybe that's why it was so nervous when I went in." Gayle set her glass carefully in the sink. "It really scared me, Steph. I don't *ever* want to be scared like that again. But . . ."

Stephanie frowned. "But what?"

For a moment Gayle couldn't speak. She stared at Stephanie; she could feel herself trembling again.

"But I'm afraid I'm going to be," she whispered.

A troubled silence settled between them. Gayle could see the concern in Stephanie's eyes . . . could see Stephanie getting up and walking toward her.

Stephanie sighed. "You're so *weird.*" She gave Gayle a quick hug, then put her hands on Gayle's shoulders and steered her from the room. "Go upstairs. Take a shower. Put on your nightgown. Get unconscious. Quit making me crazy."

"I'm sorry." Gayle made a weak attempt at laughter. "I don't know why I said that. I'm just really tired."

"I know. Me, too. So which rooms are we using?"

Gayle motioned to the doorway at the top of the stairs. "I've always used that one. Take your pick."

"As far from you as possible. So I can sleep late and not hear you being cheerful in the morning."

"The one at the end of the hall, then. Aunt Pat's room is here on this floor."

"Great. Go take your shower. Leave me in peace."

Together they hauled their stuff upstairs. Gayle showed Stephanie around, then went into her own room and opened her suitcase on the bed. She could hear Stephanie getting settled down the hall, the blare of Stephanie's radio coming on. Gayle checked the clock on the dresser and frowned. Seven-thirty. What could be taking Aunt Pat so long?

She crossed restlessly to the window and peered out. The old maple was still there, towering high above the rooftop, one of its thick branches touching the house, several smaller limbs brushing leaves against her windowpane. On this side of the yard the trees had practically taken over, extending out to meet the natural woods that covered the hills as far as she could see. When she was little, Gayle had loved going with Aunt Pat on exploring expeditions, but now the woods looked strangely sinister.

She started to draw the curtains, then stopped with a frown. *What happened to the screen?* Aunt

Pat had always been fussy about window screens, living way out here in the country. *Can't be too careful,* she'd always said. *Those darn mosquitoes would just love to carry me off while I sleep!* But there wasn't a screen on the window now, and Gayle made a mental note to ask about it later.

She yanked the curtains shut. Aunt Pat would laugh at her for that—after all, they were miles from the nearest neighbor—but Gayle felt a lot more secure knowing *nothing* could see inside.

She thought about the arm they'd found.

She leaned into the curtains, her forehead resting on the windowpane. She just couldn't wait anymore . . . she had to tell someone about it—

She went back downstairs and found the number of the sheriff's office. The phone rang and rang—four times . . . seven. Just as she was about to hang up, someone finally answered.

"Sheriff's office," a woman mumbled.

"Yes . . . hi . . . ummm . . ." Gayle's mind went blank. She paused a moment, trying to decide what to say.

"Hello?" the voice said impatiently. "Is anyone there?"

"Hi, yes, I don't live here, but I'm visiting my aunt, and I wanted to report something in a garbage dump—"

"Look, honey, I don't have time for this right now. If someone's trespassing on your property or burning trash without a permit, you'll have to stop by and file a complaint, okay?"

"No, that's not what I meant—I mean, it's not my dump—it's a dump by the road—"

"Well, it's just gonna have to wait, you hear what I'm saying? The sheriff's out on an emergency, and all hell's breaking loose over here. Why don't you call back tomorrow?"

The phone clicked and went dead. Gayle stared at the receiver for a minute, then replaced it and went back upstairs.

She could hear Stephanie singing in the room down the hall—singing as though nothing had ever happened. *Well, I tried to tell someone,* Gayle argued with herself. *It's not my fault if nobody wants to listen. . . .*

It'd be different when Aunt Pat got home, she reminded herself firmly. Aunt Pat knew everybody in Pine Ridge—Aunt Pat would know just who to call.

She closed her eyes, fighting off the image of that black, blistered skin . . . the bony skeleton fingers with the flesh missing . . . the deep, black shadows in the barn . . .

Maybe I really did imagine something in the barn, she tried to reason with herself. After all, ever since they'd gotten to the house she'd been so nervous and jumpy. . . .

Something cold slid over her shoulder, and Gayle whirled around with a scream.

"What!" Stephanie shouted. "What's wrong!"

"Stephanie!" Gayle shouted back. "For God's sake, you scared me to death!"

"*You?* What about *me?*"

"I didn't hear you come in! And your hands are like ice!"

"Sorry. I washed them in cold water, 'cause it's so *hot* up here."

"That's cause the air conditioners are downstairs," Gayle said. "Maybe if we turn on the attic fan, it'll help."

"I'm gonna die," Stephanie groaned.

Gayle sat down on the edge of the bed. Stephanie plopped down beside her.

"You're not going to die." Gayle hid a smile. "Is that all you came in here to tell me?"

"No, I wanted to show you this newspaper. It was on the hamper in the bathroom."

"So?"

"So"—Stephanie chuckled—"this small-town stuff really cracks me up. Not to mention the great journalistic style."

Gayle threw her a look. "Okay, I'm ready. Read it to me."

Stephanie unfolded the paper and smoothed it over her knees. Bending forward, she pointed at the bottom of the page.

"This article down here." Her voice dropped, her tone going dramatic. " 'Who *is* the Pine Ridge Stalker?' "

"The what?"

"Will you pay attention?" Stephanie scolded. "Stalker. The Pine Ridge Stalker." She cleared her throat, shifting into dramatic mode once more. " 'Who *is* the Pine Ridge Stalker? Does he live among us, unsuspected, unnoticed, as one of our neighbors? Or has he disappeared forever, just like the helpless victims he preys upon?' "

Gayle's smile was uneasy. "Sounds like some kind of legend to me."

"That's not all." Stephanie shook the paper at her. "There's a poem—listen:

"He sees in the dark,
  He prowls in the night,
  But maybe he's one of your friends
  In the light,
  And maybe he'll watch you
  And maybe he'll wait
  And maybe you'll trust him . . .
  Until it's too *late.*"

Stephanie ended with a theatrical whisper. As Gayle stared at her, she giggled and lay back on the bed.

"Can you imagine *our* newspaper printing garbage like this?" she demanded.

"It's not funny, Steph," Gayle said quietly.

"Of course it's funny. It's obvious somebody wrote it as a joke—"

"How do you know?" Gayle demanded.

"Well, who in their right mind could ever take this poem seriously?"

"I don't think stalkers are anything to joke about."

"You don't even know what the Pine Ridge Stalker is!"

"Well, what is he, then?" Gayle frowned. "What else does the article say about him?"

Stephanie crumpled the paper and tossed it at Gayle's head. "Nothing. I guess everybody already knows about the Stalker but us." She sat up again and watched as Gayle rummaged in the suitcase. "What's wrong with you, anyway?"

"I don't know." Gayle's look was annoyed. "I guess finding an arm just doesn't put me in the best of moods."

"Then call the police and quit worrying about it!"

"Well, why isn't Aunt Pat home?"

"I don't know!"

Tempers rising, the two friends glared at each other. After a moment Gayle turned abruptly and began gathering her things together for the bathroom.

"I'm going to take my shower," she mumbled. "You can watch TV downstairs, if you want."

"Fine. And since I'm still starving, can I have some of that country gourmet sausage quiche, too, if I want?"

"Fine."

And *this is so silly,* Gayle thought to herself as she locked the bathroom door. *We're making each other mad just so we won't have to think about what we found back there at that garbage dump. . . .*

She stayed in the shower a long time. She kept telling herself she'd get out in five more minutes, and that when she finally did, Aunt Pat would be home and there'd be nothing at all to worry about. They'd hug and laugh and sit down at the kitchen table, and then the three of them would plan out all the fun they were going to have for the next two weeks. She tried not to think of the other things. She tried not to think about them, and she tried to pretend they hadn't happened.

At last Gayle turned off the water. She slid open the shower door and toweled herself off, then slipped into her nightgown. The bathroom swirled with steam. It curled out ahead of her as she opened the door, filling the hallway like soft gray smoke.

"Steph!" she called. "I'm finished if you want to use the bathroom!"

She was sorry they'd snapped at each other. She could hear the TV blaring from the living room, and she smiled to herself as she threw her clothes on the bed.

Just like Stephanie. She probably ate all my quiche—plus ten more cookies—and fell asleep on the couch.

"Steph!" she yelled again. She turned out her light and hurried down the stairs. She stopped in the doorway of the living room, and she stared.

It was empty.

"Steph?" she called again. "Steph? You down here?"

Maybe she really wasn't down here, Gayle thought to herself—maybe she'd gone back upstairs while Gayle was in the shower—

"Steph?"

Frowning, Gayle walked slowly through the living room. She could see the TV remote on the couch, the smashed cushions where Steph had been sitting, Stephanie's romance novel lying open on the end table. *That's weird. . . . I wonder where she is. . . .*

"Steph, please answer me!"

Gayle jumped as a noise sounded from the back of the house. *A door? Was that a door closing?* She stood for a minute trying to decide what she'd actually heard, and then she wandered slowly past the couch and into the dining room. She could see the doorway now that led to the kitchen; she could smell the faint aroma of food.

"Don't try to hide it, Steph—I know you've finished off every bit of my quiche!"

Laughing, she hurried into the kitchen. She walked through the door, and then she froze, a scream lodging silently in her throat.

She saw the stranger kneeling on the floor. . . .

She saw the knife clutched in his hand.

And beside him, in a pool of blood, lay Stephanie.

5

She did scream then.

She screamed Stephanie's name, and the intruder looked up in surprise, so that she could really see his face.

To Gayle's horror, she realized she'd seen him before.

Earlier, on the road, when she and Stephanie had backed into his truck.

"Get a towel," he told her.

Gayle stood paralyzed as he jumped to his feet and threw the knife into the sink. She saw him roll Stephanie gently onto her side—she saw the dark flash of anger on his face.

"A towel!" he yelled. "Get me a towel, dammit! You want her to bleed to death?"

Gayle didn't even remember pulling the dishtowel from the rack by the door; suddenly she was just holding it out to him, and he was snatching it away. Stephanie's white T-shirt was red with blood, and as Gayle fought down a sudden wave of nausea, she saw the young man carefully press the towel against Stephanie's stomach. Gayle's scream was still stuck in her throat, choking her. She could see the phone on the other side of the room, but she had to get past the stranger to reach it.

"Come on," he said gruffly. He stood up, lifting Stephanie in his arms. The back door was already open, but he kicked it wider. "Well, come *on!*" he said again. "Let's get her into the truck!"

He was outside now, and at last Gayle reached for the phone. He paused and turned back to scowl at her.

"Forget 911," he told her. "This'll be faster."

Numbly Gayle followed him. The pickup was parked next to the house, and he threw open the door.

"Well, get in!" he shouted.

"Where are you taking her?"

"To the hospital! Are you coming or staying?"

Gayle climbed in. The young man eased Stephanie across her lap, then ran around to the driver's side. Gayle's head was spinning—she couldn't think—*couldn't think!* As they backed toward the road, she wrapped her arms around Stephanie and held her tightly, but her friend felt lifeless.

"Why?" Gayle mumbled. Her numbness was beginning to thaw now—her mind was beginning to work. She turned slightly to stare at him. "Why are you doing this?"

His face was hidden in shadows, yet she felt his eyes upon her, a brief, unmistakable coldness before he glanced away again. He pressed harder on the accelerator. His body was tense, as tense as his voice when he finally answered.

"You don't want her to die, do you?" the young man mumbled.

"What did you do to her?"

She felt his glance again. She felt the coldness linger this time before his eyes returned to the road.

"You think I did this to her." It was a statement, not a question. Calm. Matter of fact.

Gayle said nothing. He shifted gears, and the truck lurched forward, shooting around a hairpin curve. She closed her eyes and held Stephanie closer.

"Hang on, Steph," she whispered. "Just hang on."

"Keep that tight against her," he ordered.

"Can't you go any faster?"

"Not if you want us all to live."

Silence fell between them. Minutes dragged by. Gayle felt as if she were trapped in a nightmare with no escape.

"I found her like that," she heard him say at last.

Gayle opened her eyes and stared at his chiseled profile. She saw one of his hands clench on the steering wheel.

"I found her like this," he said again. "I came in, and she was on the floor."

Gayle gave a vague nod. She felt warm and sticky, and there was that metallic smell of blood, so strong now in the truck, and from some remote part of her brain she thought how furious Stephanie would be, getting her favorite T-shirt all bloody. . . .

"When?" she heard herself ask. "When did you find her?"

"Just before you came in. She was lying there with the knife in her."

Gayle's brain was spinning again, trying to keep up, trying to sort it out and make sense of everything. Was he telling the truth? *He must be telling the truth—he doesn't even know us—why would he want to hurt Stephanie?*

"Who are you?" she asked. "What were you doing in our house?"

"Your house? I could ask you the same thing—"

"It's my aunt's house. I'm *supposed* to be there."

"Your . . ." His voice trailed off. This time his head turned slightly as he gave her a quick appraisal. "Then . . . you must be Gayle?"

Gayle nodded stiffly. "Aunt Pat wasn't home when we got there. What's going on?"

"She's in Evanston. She won't be back till tomorrow night."

Gayle shook her head slightly. "And *who* are you?"

"Travis McGraw. I do work around your aunt's place."

"Oh. I . . ." Gayle took a deep breath and leaned her head back against the seat. "I guess I don't know about you. Aunt Pat never mentioned you."

"That doesn't surprise me. A lot of things seem to slip her mind these days."

Gayle looked down at her lap, at Stephanie's pale face. "Why would someone do this?" she whispered. Her voice broke, and she took a deep breath. "Why would someone deliberately break in and stab her—"

"Nobody did," Travis said mildly.

"What do you mean?"

45

"She did it herself. She fell on the knife."

"What!"

"Are you holding that tight enough?"

"Yes. Yes, I think so," Gayle assured him, though she didn't really have any feeling in her fingers anymore. She looked down again into Stephanie's face. "Steph," she whispered. "Oh, Steph . . . what happened . . . ?"

"I saw her," Travis said grimly. "Through the window at the top of the door. I could see her doubled over . . . staggering with the knife in her hand. I was trying to get the door open, and by the time I got in, she was already on the floor. I was just checking her when you showed up."

Silently Gayle stared at him. *He must be telling the truth, he must be.* There was blood on his workshirt, on his rolled-up sleeves and bare forearms. A streak of blood on one cheek where he'd wiped it with his hand. *But I don't know him, and Aunt Pat never said anything about him—I don't even know if he really works for her or not—but he said that a lot of things slip Aunt Pat's mind, and isn't that why I'm here, 'cause we're afraid maybe she's getting senile—so he must be telling the truth about that. . . .*

She wished Aunt Pat were here now to give her some answers. She wished she and Stephanie hadn't made this stupid trip. She wished her head didn't feel as if it were going to explode—

"That doesn't make sense." The sound of her own voice startled her. "How could she have *fallen* on it?"

Travis shrugged. "Was she sick? Does she have dizzy spells? Anything like that?"

46

Gayle shook her head. "She's as strong as a horse."

"Maybe she was tired . . . or needed to eat—"

"She's *been* eating. We've both been eating all day long and—"

She broke off abruptly. She wished they hadn't argued about all those stupid things. If anything happened to Stephanie . . .

"Hey, come on," Travis said. "She'll be okay."

"I should have been with her. Maybe it wouldn't have happened."

He didn't answer. The truck bounced and swerved over rutted country roads, and Gayle wondered if they'd ever make it to town. After what seemed like forever, she finally heard Travis mumble, "We're almost there," and two minutes later she spotted bright lights and a hospital sign ahead of them.

The truck roared up to a covered walkway and jerked to a stop. Expecting Travis to jump out at once, Gayle was surprised when he simply sat there staring at the building. The thought ran through her mind that maybe he didn't like hospitals and was reluctant to go inside, but before she could say anything, he got out and went in through a door marked EMERGENCY. Almost immediately a team of medical workers flew out with a gurney, hoisted Stephanie onto it, and hurried her away.

Gayle still felt dazed. She kept staring down at her bloodstained clothes and hardly realized that Travis was helping her out of the truck.

"Here," he said. "Put this on."

"What?"

"You might feel more comfortable," he said offhandedly.

She stared at the denim jacket he was holding out to her—then it hit her that she was still in her nightgown. A hot blush crept over her cheeks. She mumbled a thank you and wriggled into the jacket, then followed him into the waiting room.

There were several nurses behind the front desk . . . several doctors and orderlies moving in different directions through hallways that opened off the small waiting room. The first thing Gayle noticed was that they were all looking at Travis. Some of them stopped walking to turn and stare; others shot him quick, furtive glances as if they thought he wouldn't notice. If he did notice, he didn't let on. Instead he strode over to the desk and started talking to the nurses while Gayle stood there uneasily.

"Stand clear—coming through."

Startled, Gayle jumped back as an empty wheelchair rolled past her. The young man pushing it glanced over and gave her a wink, letting his eyes travel deliberately down to her feet and back up again. For the second time Gayle felt her cheeks grow warm. He looked about the same age as Travis—nineteen or twenty, she thought—and though he was wearing an orderly's uniform, he looked as if he'd just stepped from the pages of a fashion catalog. His brown hair was combed neatly, every strand in place, and his charming smile and hazel eyes shone with total self-assurance. Passing her, he stopped the wheelchair next to Travis and tossed a chart onto the desk. Travis didn't even look his way.

"What's going on?" the orderly asked.

"Stab wound," the nurse murmured. "They need you in three."

The boy's lips curled in a smile, though it seemed almost mocking. "Up to your handiwork again, McGraw?"

It seemed to Gayle that Travis's shoulders tightened, yet he didn't turn around or respond. The nurses exchanged worried looks. The orderly laughed softly and steered the wheelchair away, disappearing down one of the corridors.

Not knowing what else to do, Gayle sat down in the waiting area. She could see the nurses eyeing her curiously as Travis spoke to them. She stared down at the floor. After a while she saw Travis's boots stop in front of her, and as she looked up, he held out a Styrofoam cup.

"Coffee?"

It was too hot for coffee and she'd never liked it anyway, but she nodded and took the cup. Travis slouched down in the chair beside her and gazed at a spot on the far wall.

"Do I have to talk to someone—fill out papers or something?" she asked, but he shook his head.

"We can take care of all that later. I told them who you are and where you're staying—they all know your aunt."

"Small town, I keep forgetting." She tried to smile, but her lips seemed frozen. He *had* to be telling the truth about Stephanie, she kept telling herself—after all, if he'd tried to commit murder, why would he hang around to make sure Stephanie was safe?

"You don't have to stay," she said at last.

"I know."

As they both continued to sit and wait, Gayle could see those same wary looks the nurses shot them from time to time, but again, if Travis noticed them, he gave no sign.

Time dragged on. The waiting room was very quiet, and no one else came in. Gayle heard the muffled tones of the nurses at the desk, the whisper of footsteps, the rustle of uniforms—and after a while all the noises blended together in her head. She was halfway aware of nodding off, and then of her coffee cup being gently pried from her hand.

"Gayle?" a voice said.

Slowly she opened her eyes, struggling to remember where she was. As she blinked herself awake, she realized she was leaning on Travis's shoulder and immediately jerked upright.

"Gayle, this is Dr. Maxwell," Travis said, getting to his feet. Gayle started to stand as well, but the doctor motioned her to stay put and sat down in Travis's chair.

"Hello, Gayle." Dr. Maxwell gave her hand a perfunctory shake. "Your aunt and I are good friends. I've been out to the farm quite a lot for those dizzy spells of hers."

Gayle looked at Travis. His arms were crossed over his chest, and his face was grim.

"You could say I *inherited* Pat when old Doc Yates retired a few years back," Dr. Maxwell went on. "He said it'd be good for his patients to have a younger doctor—unfortunately, he never warned me how stubborn a lot of them could be—*especially* your aunt." He paused . . . gave a brief

50

smile. "Or how sweet and generous. In fact, sometimes too generous for her own good."

Was it her imagination or did he seem tense and guarded, Gayle wondered—*just like those nurses, just like everyone else in this weird place. . . .*

"How's my friend?" Gayle asked.

"She'll be fine," Dr. Maxwell assured her. "The knife wound was deep, but not so serious—no organ damage, we can be grateful for that."

Again he hesitated. He glanced up at Travis. Travis was staring at the front door, his features hard like stone.

"You know I'll have to report this" Dr. Maxwell sounded uncomfortable. "I'm sorry, Travis."

"Do what you have to do" was all Travis said.

"What's he talking about?" Gayle asked, but Travis wouldn't answer. "Report what to who? Are you talking about the police?"

"Well . . . with cases like this . . . if something looks the least bit suspicious—" the doctor began, but Travis cut him off.

"That's a lie, and you know it."

"It's policy—" the doctor tried again, but again Travis broke in.

"*New* policy, you mean. If it involves *me,* you mean—"

"Look, Travis, there's no need for any trouble—"

"There's nothing suspicious about this—my friend fell on that knife!" Gayle burst out. "I don't know what you two are talking about, but it was an accident. She doubled over, and then she . . . she fell."

Travis and Dr. Maxwell were both staring at her now. She could see suspicion on both their faces, and she could hear herself babbling, but she couldn't seem to stop.

"If it hadn't been for Travis, my friend might have died. He's the one who brought us here—he's the one who saved her."

Travis's eyes dropped to the floor. A moment of silence passed before the doctor spoke again.

"Did you *see* her fall on the knife?" he asked.

Gayle met his stare with a level one of her own. "Yes. I was just coming into the kitchen, but she fell before I could get to her."

The doctor's eyes never left her face. Finally he nodded, though Gayle thought it seemed reluctant. "She has a severe case of food poisoning," he admitted. "And it's not unusual for stomach spasms to become quite violent—"

"Food poisoning?" Gayle broke in, and Dr. Maxwell leaned toward her.

"What exactly has she eaten today—do you know?"

Gayle's mind raced. "Oh . . . well . . . lots of things. I mean, it was a ten-hour drive, and we stopped a lot along the way. Hamburgers, sodas, fries, some candy bars, I think. Those little orange crackers with peanut butter . . . doughnuts—"

"Did both of you eat the same food?"

"Pretty much. Till we got to Aunt Pat's. I haven't eaten anything since then, but Steph has. Cookies. Oh—and quiche. Aunt Pat's sausage quiche."

"How long ago?"

"I'm not sure. . . ."

"How long before she got sick?"

"Half an hour, maybe?"

The doctor seemed to be weighing all the facts. He shook his head slowly, then stood up again. He turned his back to Travis and rested a hand on Gayle's shoulder.

"We've given her medication and run some blood work, just to be safe. We'll have the results sometime tomorrow, but she'll have to stay a few days. We need to keep an eye on that wound."

"Can I see her?"

"Not now, she's sleeping. If you could come back tomorrow—"

"No, please let me stay with her now," Gayle interrupted. "She's my best friend—if she wakes up in a strange place and I'm not here—"

"I understand how you feel." The doctor's tone softened a little. "Having loved ones in the hospital is a scary thing. We'll make sure someone's with her." He gave Gayle's arm a professional pat and finally looked back at Travis. "Are you taking her home?"

Travis nodded.

"Then I assume you'll be around just in case anyone needs to talk with you?"

No nod this time. Only that stony stare.

"I'm sorry, Travis," the doctor said again, not looking sorry at all. "I don't have a choice in this."

Travis watched silently as Dr. Maxwell walked away. Then he slowly crumpled his empty cup in one fist.

"What's going on?" Gayle asked, whirling around to face him. "What was he talking about?"

"Wait outside," Travis said.

"No. I want to find out what's—"

"And don't lie for me. I don't need your help, and you don't have any business getting involved in this—"

"In what? Why is everyone watching you? What's—"

"Just go wait in the car."

His voice was cold and angry. Without another word he turned and walked back to the desk, and after a moment of indecision, Gayle did as he'd told her. She was starting to feel sick again, and thoughts were racing like mad through her head. Why was Travis such an object of stares and suspicion? And why *had* she jumped to his defense like that, when she didn't even know what was going on?

She stepped off the walkway and scanned the parking lot. There weren't many cars out here, but there were several pickup trucks, and she had no idea which one belonged to Travis. She leaned back against the building and pressed a hand to her forehead. She could feel a headache coming on, and the heat out here was stifling. A mosquito landed on her neck, and she slapped it away.

She thought about her parents and what they'd be doing back home. She'd promised to call tonight, to let them know she and Stephanie had gotten here safely. So what was she going to do now? *Oh, hi, everyone, Aunt Pat's not here and Steph's in the hospital with a stab wound in her stomach, and there's this guy I met that nobody seems to like, and oh, by the way, Steph got food poisoning, too. . . .*

You'll have to lie. The answer came to her clearly,

and she gave a humorless smile. Of course she'd have to lie—what else could she do?

A grisly scene began to form in her mind—the garbage dump and the laundry bag and the burnt arm reaching out toward her—*like it wanted me to help, like it wanted me to tell someone. . . .* A fresh wave of guilt pounded over her. *But I did try to tell the sheriff and nobody would listen—what else can I do?*

She thought about those blackened fingers. . . .

That article in the paper about the Pine Ridge Stalker . . .

The way everyone had watched Travis in the emergency room tonight . . . those mysterious insinuations Dr. Maxwell had made . . .

Something's going on around here—something bad—I just wish I knew what it was.

What was taking Travis so long, anyway? She felt nervous out here in the parking lot all by herself. There was only one streetlight working, and thick shadows gathered everywhere . . . crouching behind trucks . . . oozing beneath cars . . .

This is crazy. I'm going inside.

She pushed off from the wall, then stopped abruptly as a faint noise came from overhead. It was a halting, scraping sort of sound . . . like a window being slowly and carefully opened . . . yet as Gayle peered up at the three stories of windows, all she could see was darkness.

Despite the heat, a cold prickling went over her skin. As though she were being watched . . . as though invisible eyes were hiding up there in the shadows.

Again she let her gaze travel across the face of the building. For just a second she thought there might have been a slight movement from one of the second-floor windows—one just slightly to the left of where she was standing—but as she squinted and tried to focus in on it, she realized it was only a small flock of birds roosting on the outside ledge.

Gayle sighed in relief.

She forced herself to look down again. She forced herself to take a step.

Above her the birds took sudden flight, filling the air with a startled flurry of wings. As Gayle glanced up in surprise, she saw the quick shifting of shadows beyond the window ledge—the dark outline of something plunging toward her—

She tried to get out of the way.

She tried to turn and run, but there was only a sickening thud against her skull, and the silent roar of darkness.

 **6**

"Is she okay?"

Gayle thought she knew the voice.

Soft and distant, she could hear it speaking, and she sensed it had something to do with her. She tried to concentrate . . . tried to identify it . . . tried to answer, but a dense fog filled her head, and she couldn't seem to fight her way through.

"Is she okay?" the voice spoke again.

Yes, I'm okay, of course I'm okay. Can someone hear me? Who's there?

Again Gayle struggled to make herself heard, but there were more voices now—harsh and jarring— voices she *didn't* know, and she wished they'd all be quiet and just let her float along in the nice, peaceful fog. . . .

"She's coming to. Gayle? This is Dr. Maxwell. Can you hear me?"

Not the voice. Not the voice I heard first . . .

Gayle felt herself frown. A wave of agony washed

over her, and she moaned and groped out, trying to find her head. Someone took both her hands. After struggling weakly for several seconds, she finally opened her eyes.

A hazy circle of faces swam above her. *Like shadows along the front of a building . . .*

"Window," Gayle mumbled. "Someone was in that window."

She grimaced as more pain stabbed through her head. Slowly she tried to raise up, but she couldn't use her arms.

"Gayle, do you know where you are?" Dr. Maxwell asked calmly.

"I think he threw something at me," Gayle went on. "Because the birds flew up and . . ."

The faces came into sharp focus, and her voice trailed away. Dr. Maxwell . . . a nurse . . . that orderly she'd seen earlier in the waiting room . . . and Travis. Travis holding both her hands.

"Do you know where you are?" Dr. Maxwell repeated patiently.

Gayle looked from one face to another. She pulled free from Travis's grasp.

"At the hospital," she said. "Something hit me. I saw something falling—I saw him move in the window."

Everyone but Travis glanced at each other, and Gayle felt even more confused. She wished they'd say something to her instead of just passing those strange looks back and forth.

"One of the bricks came loose and hit you," Dr. Maxwell explained. "Do you understand? One of the bricks fell off the building and hit you in the head and on the shoulder. Mark found you outside."

Gayle didn't answer. She stared at the doctor and slowly shook her head.

"This just isn't your night, young lady," Dr. Maxwell said mildly. "I want to keep you here and—"

"I'm not staying," Gayle mumbled.

The looks again. All but Travis, who'd been staring at her the whole time.

"Do I have to stay?" Gayle's voice rose anxiously. "Is there some law that says I have to stay?"

"Well, of course there's no law—" the doctor began, but Gayle broke in.

"Then I'm not staying, I'm going home. I want to go home right now."

An uneasy silence hung in the air. At last Dr. Maxwell sighed and nodded curtly in Travis's direction.

"I'll send some medication with her," he said, and motioned the nurse to follow him from the room. Travis turned and went silently after them. The orderly stayed behind.

"What's the matter?" he deadpanned. "Don't like our lovely accommodations here?"

He flashed her that perfect smile, and Gayle, in spite of her pain, couldn't help smiling back.

"You're Mark?" she asked, and his smile widened.

"The one and only."

"So you're the one I should thank."

"Hey. Don't mention it. Anytime you need to be rescued, I'm your man."

He moved closer. She detected the faint scent of aftershave, along with those familiar hospital smells of rubbing alcohol and antiseptic, soap, and medicines.

"Mark what?" she mumbled.

"Gentry. And you're Gayle Nelson. Visiting your aunt Pat for two weeks."

Gayle's eyes widened in surprise. "How'd you know that?"

"Small town. News travels fast. Not to mention information at the admitting desk."

"Oh, that." Gayle sighed. "How could I forget about poor Stephanie?"

"Don't worry about your friend. I passed her room a little while ago, and she was resting comfortably, as they like to say around here. I think it's your turn to be worried about. That's quite a beauty mark you have there." He gently touched the left side of her head. "You're lucky it hit at the angle it did—it just grazed you. You could've been killed."

"Could I?" Gayle asked. "So tell me again . . . *what* happened?"

"They're renovating the other two floors in this part of the building," Mark explained. "That's why they're closed down. One of the bricks must have come loose—when I found you outside, it was on the ground beside you."

Gayle stared at him. "But someone was in the window," she said again. "I saw him when the birds flew."

"Birds? What birds?"

He was speaking calmly, yet Gayle could hear the

amusement beneath his tone. It was obvious he didn't believe her.

"I thought I heard something." She sighed again and closed her eyes. "Like a window opening, only I couldn't see anything. Until I noticed the birds on the windowsill. And then they flew up, and I saw someone."

Mark was silent for several seconds. Finally he said, "But there wouldn't have been anyone up there, right? 'Cause the place is off-limits to everybody but workmen—and they're never here at night. Are you sure you really saw someone? Could it have been shadows, maybe?"

Gayle's mind raced back. *Shadows . . . yes . . . The place was full of shadows. . . .*

"And anyway," Mark went on casually, "this guy in the window—if there really *was* a guy in the window—the way you're talking about him, sounds almost like you think he *threw* the brick at you." Mark stopped . . . folded his arms across his chest . . . fixed his eyes on her. "Is *that* what you're saying?"

Gayle's head was racing again. She couldn't think—*didn't want* to think—it was too much in one day—too much in one night—

"Of course not," she mumbled. "Even if someone was up there, they probably didn't even see the brick fall."

"Yeah, probably not." Mark nodded. He smiled at her, that charming, melt-your-heart smile. "How come Travis wasn't with you?"

Gayle tried to think back. She was so tired . . . so tired . . .

"Where was Travis?" Mark persisted.

"I don't know. He told me to wait outside."

Again Mark nodded. He unfolded his arms and stepped toward the door. Voices were approaching from the hall, and after a quick glance into the corridor, he shot a look over his shoulder at Gayle.

"You seem like a nice girl," he said in a low voice. "Maybe you should think about keeping better company."

To Gayle's surprise he turned on his heel and strode out, pointedly ignoring Travis as they squeezed side by side through the doorway.

1

Travis was silent as they started home. Gayle stared dully out her window, watching the lights in town grow farther and farther apart until they disappeared altogether. Her head was killing her. She held one hand against it, trying to cushion it as best she could from the bumpy ride.

"Sorry," Travis mumbled.

His voice was so low that Gayle turned toward him, just to make sure she hadn't imagined it.

"About what?" she asked.

"They don't give too much attention to roads around here."

Gayle managed a smile. "That's okay. I know you're doing the best you can."

Travis didn't answer. She gazed at his stony profile and tried to think of something to say.

"Thanks for helping us tonight," she offered at last. "There's no telling what might have happened if you hadn't found Stephanie when you did."

Travis only shrugged. "You'd have found her sooner or later."

"But maybe *too* late."

Just thinking of the scene in the kitchen made her shudder all over again. She braced herself as the truck lurched over some deep ruts, then jerked slowly up an incline. She clenched her teeth and tried to ignore the pain.

After another lengthy silence, Travis murmured, "So why'd you lie?"

Gayle didn't answer at first. She thought about it for several minutes, then finally sighed. "To tell you the truth, I don't know. Partly because I suspected you, I guess. I felt really sorry about that."

She expected some sort of comment, but Travis didn't reply. Gayle pondered several more minutes before going on.

"Aunt Pat mentioned she had someone helping her, but she never told me anything about you—not even your name. I didn't know who you were when I first saw you—I'm sorry about the way I acted . . . what I said."

"Forget it," Travis said gruffly.

"No, it was wrong to jump to conclusions like that. I didn't know what to think when I saw Stephanie lying there." Gayle closed her eyes, her mind whirling back over all the events of their trip. "After everything else that happened today—I mean, we got lost and we were both so tired, and then we hit your truck, and then when I found that arm, God, it was so awful, and I tried to call the police, but nobody would listen, and then Aunt Pat wasn't there and—"

"Wait."

Gayle opened her eyes to see Travis staring at her.

"Found *what?*" he asked. "Did you say you found an arm?"

Gayle stared back at him in confusion. *The arm?* Had she really said that? She hadn't meant to—she hadn't meant to tell anyone but Aunt Pat—but she was exhausted, and somehow it had just slipped out.

"What arm?" Travis asked again, and Gayle took a deep breath. She had to tell someone. It didn't seem right to forget about it, just because the sheriff hadn't been interested—and maybe Travis would know what to do. At least she'd feel better sharing it with *someone.*

"Okay," she began, "I know this sounds really crazy, but after we hit your truck, we stopped at this roadside stand to fix our car. And I was looking around, trying to find some rope, and there was this garbage dump. I saw this sack sort of under a mattress, and the top had come open a little and—" She broke off, feeling that same cold shiver creeping over her again. "This arm was sticking out. Or . . . what was left of it."

Travis's eyes were fixed on the windshield now. There was no surprise on his face . . . no emotion in his voice.

"You're sure it was an arm?" he asked softly.

Gayle nodded.

"And *where* did you find it?"

"In a garbage dump or something—"

"No, I mean *where.* Where'd you stop?"

"I don't know. Down the road from where we hit

65

you. There was this fruit stand, but it didn't look like anyone had used it for a long time."

She thought Travis might have nodded. "I think I know the place you're talking about," he mumbled.

"We didn't know what to do—we decided to tell Aunt Pat about it, but she wasn't home when we got there, so I tried to tell the police—"

"Tried to tell them?"

"Yes. I called the sheriff's office, but the woman who answered said there wasn't anyone there, and could I call again tomorrow."

"So . . ." Travis said slowly, "you didn't tell anyone else about it?"

"No. Just Stephanie. And now you."

"Good." There was no mistaking the relief in his tone, and as Gayle shot him a curious glance, Travis added, "Don't say anything to anybody."

"Why not?" she demanded. "What about the sheriff? Shouldn't he know?"

"I don't think," he said slowly, "that Sheriff Hodges is a guy you'd enjoy talking to."

"Why not?"

"He's a bully. He loves to harass people— especially women—and I guarantee he'll make your life miserable."

"Why would he do that? I'd be helping him if I told him about it—I'd think he'd be grateful."

Travis made a derisive sound in his throat. "Grateful? For one thing, he'll want to know why you didn't report it right away. And it won't matter what you say, he'll give you the third degree about it. He'll drag your aunt in, and he'll hang around the hospital bothering your friend. Hell, he might even try to suggest *you've* got something to do with it, since you didn't tell anyone when you should have."

The pain in her head was getting worse. Gayle closed her eyes once more and tried to block out Travis's voice, tried to block out the waves of worry and exhaustion that were sweeping over her.

"But I *did* try to tell him," she insisted.

"Doesn't matter. He'll say you should have come into the office."

"Well . . . well, then . . . could *you* tell him?" She felt totally drained. She rubbed her head. She kept her eyes closed.

"I mean, if you really *want* to talk to him," Travis went on, "that's your decision, it's sure no concern of mine—"

"Could you tell him?" Gayle asked again. "Please?"

She didn't want to open her eyes. She wanted to sleep for a long, long time and wake up again in her own bed at home where this vacation was nothing more than a bad dream.

"I could," Travis said at last. "Yeah. I could, I guess, if you wanted me to."

"I want you to."

The silence stretched out. It stretched out and went on and on, as though he were thoroughly considering every angle of this arrangement. Reluctantly Gayle opened her eyes to see him watching her.

"But you can't tell anyone else," he instructed again. "If it gets back to the sheriff, you'll have the same problem."

"So what are you going to tell him, exactly?"

"I'll think of something," Travis assured her. "Don't worry about it."

He turned his attention back to the road. They were on the final stretch now, the narrow dirt lane leading to Aunt Pat's farmhouse. Feeling immensely relieved, Gayle settled back into the seat.

"So where'd you say my aunt is?" she asked him.

"Evanston."

"Where's that?"

"About a hundred fifty miles from here."

"But why? She knew we were coming today— she even left a note for us."

"Note? What note?"

"Yes. It said 'Be back soon.'"

"Oh." He hesitated a second, then added, "Well . . . I left that."

"You did?"

"I had to run some errands yesterday, before she left."

"So why'd she go to Evanston?"

"Auctions. There were a bunch of auctions scheduled from early this morning till late tonight. I talked her into going yesterday and staying over. So she wouldn't have to drive after dark."

"That doesn't sound like Aunt Pat. She loves driving in the dark."

Travis shot her a sidelong glance, then asked, "How long's it been since you've seen her?"

"Three years."

"Then you might be surprised at some things. She gets . . . you know . . . absentminded."

"Well, what about those dizzy spells Dr. Maxwell was talking about? How bad are they?"

"She tries to ignore them," Travis said evasively. "She's determined not to let old age slow her down. But the truth of it is, she's not as independent as she'd like to be."

*Just what Dad said. Go see how Aunt Pat **really** is.*

"It's just not like her to go off when she knew I was coming," Gayle said firmly.

"Well, she *didn't* forget about that—in fact, she told me you'd be here today. That's why I was coming in the house tonight—to check on you. I saw the lights, but nobody answered when I knocked at the front door."

"The TV was on," Gayle remembered. "I guess we didn't hear you."

Another long moment of silence. At last he said, "Your aunt didn't tell me your friend was coming with you."

"She didn't know. Steph didn't want to go on vacation with her parents, and at the very last second we talked them into letting her come with me. I tried to call Aunt Pat yesterday, but I guess she'd already left. I knew she wouldn't mind, though."

Travis didn't comment. Gayle stared vacantly out her window, out at the thick, black night.

"That guy at the hospital," she murmured. "Mark Gentry?"

"What about him?" Travis answered curtly.

"Do you two know each other?"

"Not if we can help it."

"Why? What's wrong with him?"

"Don't you ever get tired of asking questions?"

Gayle's mouth opened, then closed again. She hadn't expected an icy response like that, so she turned back to her window and kept still the rest of the way.

Travis pulled up to the house and stopped the truck. He reached across her and shoved open her door.

"If you need me, my number's by the phone in the kitchen."

"But don't you live here?" Gayle asked, surprised. She hadn't counted on staying in the house alone tonight. Not after Stephanie's accident . . . not after finding that arm . . .

"I'm only the hired help," Travis said abruptly. "I'm in the cabin behind the barn."

"Right. Of course." Flustered, she climbed out, then glanced down at her jacket. "Oh, I almost forgot. Here."

"Give it to me later." He glanced up into the hot, cloudless sky. "I won't need it for at least three more months."

She watched as the truck inched forward up the drive. Then suddenly he stopped again and peered out at her, frowning.

"Your aunt said you had a ponytail. And braces."

"I still wear my hair back sometimes," Gayle said, puzzled. "But the braces came off since the last time she saw me."

"And the quiche?" he asked. "Was she right about that?"

"What are you talking about?"

"Sausage quiche," he repeated, then shrugged. "She said it was your favorite. And that'd be the first thing you'd head for when you got here."

8

Gayle was too restless to sleep.

After cleaning the blood from the kitchen, she went from door to door, locking up the house, knowing how Aunt Pat would laugh at her when she found out. "Now, why would I want to lock my doors?" Aunt Pat would say. "I don't have a thing worth stealing!" But Gayle couldn't bear the thought of spending a night here feeling so vulnerable. Even if Travis *was* just right behind the barn.

Travis . . .

Gayle snuggled down on the couch and found an old black-and-white movie on TV. Even after spending time with him, she couldn't figure him out. One minute he seemed like a pretty nice guy— the next minute he was almost scary. It was hard to feel comfortable around someone when you couldn't read his expressions or his voice or even his eyes, Gayle decided. *Even if he did save Stephanie.* . . .

Reluctantly she lifted the telephone from the end

table. Her parents would be waiting for her to call, and she couldn't put it off any longer. She dialed, rehearsing what she was going to say, then let out a sigh of relief when the answering machine came on.

"Hi, Mom—hi, Dad—it's me!" She forced cheerfulness into her tone. "We're here, and we had a great trip. We're both fine. Aunt Pat's fine. Talk to you later. Bye."

Well, they weren't all lies, she told herself as she hung up the receiver. She'd call her parents again later, once Steph came home from the hospital. *It'll be all right, Steph. . . . One of these days we'll laugh about this whole stupid vacation. . . .*

Gayle glanced down at the footstool, at the crumpled newspaper Stephanie had left there. That article about the Pine Ridge Stalker . . . She'd meant to ask Travis about it, but with everything else happening, she'd completely forgotten to mention it on the way home.

Slowly she picked up the paper. She knew she shouldn't read it tonight in the house alone—it was stupid to make herself more nervous than she already was. And yet before she could stop herself, she was scanning the article again, the mysterious questions, the morbid poem. The whole thing was so weird and creepy—she wished she knew more about this Pine Ridge Stalker. Aunt Pat would probably be able to explain the whole thing tomorrow when she got home, but Gayle wanted to know tonight.

She got up and walked over to the shelves that lined both sides of the fireplace. All of Aunt Pat's favorite books were there, but the bottom shelves were stacked full of old magazines and newspapers.

Gayle dug through several piles before she had any luck. Then, spotting an interesting title, she pulled one paper free, scanned the article quickly, and carried it back to the couch.

The heading read: PINE RIDGE STALKER WILL STRIKE AGAIN. And beneath that, "Predictions by ClydaMae Wilson."

Gayle stopped and reread the author's name. In spite of the serious subject matter, she couldn't help smiling; if Stephanie were here, they'd both be cracking up. *ClydaMae Wilson . . . If that's not a small-town stereotype, I don't know what is.* Gayle decided it had to be a pseudonym, probably invented by some bored staff writer at the *Pine Ridge Gazette.* Shaking her head, she went on with the article.

Apparently ClydaMae Wilson was some sort of psychic. *Psychic? In a town like Pine Ridge?* As Gayle read further, it became clear that ClydaMae Wilson made predictions about the future, and that in this particular article she was concentrating on the Pine Ridge Stalker.

Gayle glanced up from the newspaper, letting her eyes go slowly around the living room. The windows were locked—she'd made sure of that—and the curtains were drawn, yet she had an uneasy feeling in the pit of her stomach. She didn't want to read about the Stalker, and yet she couldn't seem to stop herself—she had to go on.

Snuggling down into the cushions, Gayle turned her attention back to the paper. It was all here, she realized—everything she'd been wondering about the Pine Ridge Stalker—every frightening detail. No one knew who he was. No one had been able to offer even the slightest clue, for each of his alleged victims had vanished completely from the face of the earth. All of them had been young women, girls in their late teens. None had had any problems at home, nor any cause to run away. All had lived either in Pine Ridge or in one of the nearby towns, none more than fifty miles away. All had been sweet, fun, normal, down-to-earth girls, according to family, teachers, neighbors, and friends. And all of them had been redheads.

Gayle sat up stiffly, a stab of pain shooting through her head. She groped through the pillows for the remote and turned off the television.

All of them redheads . . .

She drew her breath in slowly . . . glanced again at the front windows. All around her the house was settling and shifting, groaning and creaking, as only old houses could do. Normally she'd have found those old sounds comforting, but now . . . tonight . . .

She made herself keep going, made herself keep reading, even though the pain in her head was getting worse. The strange disappearances had occurred ten times over the last few years, the last one being in February. . . .

This past February, Gayle realized. *Only six months ago . . .*

There'd been no leads, no clues of any kind. "The only thing we seem to agree on," Sheriff Bill Hodges was quoted as saying, "is that these girls were probably familiar with the person responsible for their disappearance." It only made sense, he went on to explain, since every community was in total panic, on the alert for strangers or suspicious activities. So when still more girls turned up missing, the logical conclusion was that they must have known—and trusted—their murderer.

Murderer. Gayle put a hand to her temple and massaged it gently. They were calling him a murderer, though no bodies had ever been found. She thought about the girls' families. The always wondering . . . the never knowing . . .

She forced herself to finish the article.

So there hadn't been a disappearance in six months now, ClydaMae Wilson reminded her readers—and the authorities were hopeful that the Stalker had grown tired of terrorizing folks in Harris County and had moved on somewhere else.

"But they're wrong," the author stated emphatically. "Dead wrong."

She predicted that the killer would strike again. Soon. Before the end of the summer.

"Maybe he's been resting," she wrote. "Renewing his strength . . . rethinking his strategy. Mingling with the rest of you on Pine Ridge's quiet streets . . . standing behind you in the checkout line at the grocery store . . . waving to your kids in the park. Maybe he's been laughing with you on your telephone . . . swimming with your kids at the pool . . . doing odd jobs around your house. And maybe he's just been waiting . . . patiently . . . waiting for his next redheaded girl."

Gayle threw the newspaper down on the floor and pulled her knees up to her chin. God, what a horrible article—what a horrible woman! She grabbed one of the pillows and clutched it tight against her chest, trying to calm her racing heart. The house was making those noises again—like the walls were breathing—raspy sounds like her own breath harsh in her throat—

Then she realized it wasn't the house at all.

It was the window.

Eyes going wide, Gayle stared at the window opposite the couch. If she stared hard enough and long enough, she could almost swear the curtains were moving—like the walls were moving—breathing, in and out, like the house seemed to be breathing around her—

Stop it—you're being totally ridiculous—stop it right now!

Slowly she got up from the couch.

Slowly she walked to the window.

I'll just reach out and take hold of those curtains—I'll just jerk them wide open—just to show myself how stupid I'm being—just to prove to myself there's nothing there. . . .

She lifted her arms from her sides . . . curled her fingers around the edges of the curtains . . .

The dark shape burst out at her without warning.

Shrieking, Gayle jumped back, curtains tangled around her flailing arms as she hit the wall.

The huge gray cat landed at her feet. It stared up at her in annoyance, then sat on the floor and proceeded to wash its face.

"Oh, God," Gayle whispered. She resisted the urge to give the cat a good, swift kick and eased down beside it instead. "Do you know what you just did to me, you stupid cat?" she muttered. "You just aged me about fifty years."

The cat regarded her blandly. It licked its paw and scratched behind one ear.

Gayle could feel her heart slowing again to its

natural rhythm. Her head felt as if it were going to split, and she clutched it between her hands. *Calm down . . . calm down . . . I told you you were being stupid. . . .* She ran one hand down the length of the curtains, patting them back into place. She watched the slow, methodical movements of the cat. She wondered if it had been here in the house all this time and just decided to come out. Otherwise . . . how had it gotten inside?

I locked everything . . . I know I did. Gayle's mind raced, mentally counting every door, every window. *Sure I did. The stupid cat must have been hiding in a closet or something.*

She got up and turned out the lights. The cat seemed oblivious to everything but its hygiene, so she left it there and went upstairs to bed.

*Steph was right . . . it **is** hot up here.* For a long time Gayle tossed and turned, then finally gave up and pushed the sheet away. She hated not having covers, but she hated sweating even more. Images kept pounding through her head—the half-burnt arm in the trash pile . . . Stephanie bleeding on the kitchen floor . . . the shadowy figure at the hospital window . . . Travis . . . Mark . . . Dr. Maxwell . . .

"Maybe he's just been waiting . . . waiting for his next redheaded girl. . . ."

The house whispered around her. She tried to picture the telephone in the kitchen and Travis's phone number right beside it—she kept telling herself that all she had to do was run downstairs and call him if she got scared. She thought about all the times at home when she'd loved having the house to herself, and how she'd never felt afraid, and how different it was tonight, here, alone.

Something made a rustling sound near her head. Starting up, she realized it was coming from inside the wall, and she choked back a scream. *Mice, probably, just mice . . .* And yet she suddenly imagined that burnt, blistered skeleton arm clawing its way through the wallpaper, trying to reach out and grab her. . . .

Gayle pulled the sheet over her head. So what if she suffocated from the heat—it was better than being scared half to death. She didn't dare tell Stephanie what a coward she was being—she'd never live it down.

At last she drifted into a fitful sleep. In her dreams she was wandering through a smoldering landfill, and hands were reaching out through the earth, trying to grab her as she ran by. She tripped over a rotting coffin and fell inside. The lid slammed down, and though she screamed at the top of her lungs, she knew no one could hear her. Frantically she began to work at the lid, scratching it with her fingernails, scratching it and clawing it, until her fingers bled, scratching and scratching and—

Gayle sat up with a cry.

She sat straight up in bed, shaking uncontrollably, sweat pouring from her body.

What had woken her—the dream? Or something else?

Slowly she pushed back the sheet and crept out of bed. She was burning up. She felt as if she was going to be sick, and she stumbled to the window to get some air.

Through a fog, she remembered her dream.

The fear and the panic.

The scratching of her nails against the lid of the coffin. *Scratching . . . scratching . . . scratching . . .*
God, it seemed so real!
She opened the curtains and fumbled for the latch.
Bleary-eyed, she peered out into the night, out into the gnarled limbs of the maple tree.
And at first she thought it was a squirrel . . . a raccoon maybe . . . something with a long furry tail that was caught on the branch right outside the screen.
Except that she couldn't really see the animal.
And the tail seemed incredibly long. . . .
Gayle rubbed her eyes and pressed her face against the glass. Moonlight angled down through the leaves, and the tail-thing seemed to ripple and glow, all soft and silky and red. . . .
Red . . .
Gayle felt the latch come free.
She saw her hands, in slow-motion, raising the window.
And somehow she knew—even before she reached out—even before she caught the long, red tail-thing between her trembling fingers . . .
It wasn't a tail at all.
It was human hair.

9

For a second the room seemed to tilt around her.

Gayle stumbled back from the window, her mouth open in a soundless scream, her hands wiping frantically at her nightgown.

Hair . . . red hair . . . no—it's impossible—

She grabbed her robe and raced down to the kitchen. Snatching up the phone, she scanned the list of numbers hanging there on the wall, but she couldn't find Travis's name anywhere—not Travis's name or anyone else's name—only unidentified numbers. In total frustration she threw the phone down and ran outside. She could see the silhouette of the barn from here, and beyond that the feeble glow of an outside light. Without another thought Gayle kept running.

The next thing she knew, the cabin was straight ahead of her, a single bulb hanging above the front stoop. She threw herself against the door, pounding with her fists and yelling at the top of her lungs.

"Travis! Travis! *Wake up!*"

The door opened almost immediately. Losing her balance, Gayle pitched forward into a pair of strong arms.

"What's wrong?" Travis demanded. "What are you doing out here?"

He was wearing jeans, but nothing else. From her precarious position, Gayle could see the way they fit him—tight and low on his narrow hips. She could feel his bare chest beneath her cheek . . . the firm warmth of his muscles. His feet were bare, too, and though he finally managed to steady her, their bodies were still touching.

"What—" he began again, but Gayle broke in shakily.

"There's something outside my window—something horrible—I know it's from those girls—"

"What girls?" Travis looked completely bewildered. "What are you talking about?"

"The Stalker!" Gayle's voice rose, and she fought back panic. "Those girls who disappeared—they all had red hair! Just like me! It was *hair,* Travis—someone put hair in the tree outside my window—"

"Stay here."

Abruptly he turned her loose. Gayle heard him rummaging in the cabin, and a second later he reappeared, brandishing a shotgun.

"Wait!" Gayle cried as he started down the path. "I'm going with you!"

"No, you're not—you're staying here. I mean it. Go inside and lock the door. And don't let anyone in."

Richie Tankersley Cusick

"But—"

"Just do it, Gayle!"

Before she could answer, he strode off toward the house. For several seconds she stood there watching him, but as he faded into the darkness, she went in and bolted the door.

This can't be happening . . . it's too insane. . . .

Gayle leaned back against the door and shut her eyes. *Deep breaths, that's right, you can do it. You have to clear your mind. You have to think straight.*

Think straight.

Her eyes opened slowly. What if that thing in the tree really *was* an animal? What if she'd been dreaming and imagined the whole thing? And why on earth had she even *mentioned* the Stalker? She didn't have a clue what that thing could be, hanging out there in the maple. And just because she'd filled her mind with horror stories just before going to bed . . .

She gave a soft moan. *Now what've I done? Running down here like a complete idiot, screaming for help like some hysterical female . . . I can't face him after this—I'm totally humiliated.*

And yet, somehow, she knew better. Deep in her heart she *knew* what she'd seen and what it was. Human hair. There was no mistaking the feel of it between her fingers. Human hair. *Red human hair.*

Gayle fixed her gaze on the interior of the cabin. It was only one room, with a bathroom opening off at the rear, and very sparsely furnished. A stone fireplace took up one wall, and a makeshift kitchen occupied one corner. Travis obviously didn't spend much time here—and he certainly didn't cook.

Gayle walked over to the fireplace. There were

82

rugs and blankets piled on the floor in front of the hearth, and she guessed this was where he slept. There was a cane-bottom rocking chair piled with dirty clothes . . . a pair of boots on the mantel. Gayle looked around for a chair, then sat down gingerly on some of the rugs. A book lay facedown on a pillow, and she picked it up. It was a book about building log cabins, and she put it down again.

Well, Travis McGraw, no one could ever accuse you of being pretentious.

Restlessly Gayle stood up again. She walked around the perimeter of the room. She kept seeing the hair hanging outside her window. . . . She kept remembering her nightmare. *Those horrible scratching sounds . . .* Now she began to wonder if she'd really dreamed them at all—or if someone else—someone *real*—had made them, tapping, tapping at the windowpane. . . .

She had to stop thinking about it. She'd go crazy if she thought about it anymore.

She scooped up the clothes from the rocking chair. To her surprise, something fell out on the floor, and when she leaned down to pick it up, she saw that it was a scrapbook.

Curious, Gayle sat down in the chair and opened the book on her lap.

She'd expected photos, something personal or slightly sentimental at the very least—but what she saw there made the blood chill in her veins.

Newspaper articles.

Page after page of clippings, ripped and haphazardly torn, some of them taped in place, others simply crammed in.

As she flipped from one to another, she realized they were all about the same thing:

The Pine Ridge Stalker.

Gayle sat there, staring. From somewhere in the back of her mind she was vaguely aware of a persistent pounding noise . . . a deep, impatient voice . . .

"Gayle? Come on, let me in."

Slowly she came to her senses. Enough to comprehend that someone was knocking on the door . . . that someone was standing just outside.

Jumping to her feet, she gasped as the book fell again, this time spilling some of its contents across the floor. As quickly as she could, she gathered them together and stuffed them back inside.

"Gayle, it's Travis. Open up."

Had they been in any special order? It was too late now to worry about that—she had to hide the book again before he came in.

"I—umm—how do I know it's really you?" she called, her mind racing.

"Quit screwing around. Open the door."

"Okay. Okay—just a minute."

She put the scrapbook back on the seat of the rocking chair. Frantically she threw the pile of dirty clothes on top, stood back to survey the job, then hurried to let Travis inside.

He didn't speak right away; he came in and shut the door behind him. Then he stood for a moment, staring at her, yet Gayle could swear that his gaze shifted past her for just an instant, over to the rocking chair in the corner.

"I don't know what you thought you saw," he said quietly. "But there's nothing in that tree."

Now it was Gayle's turn to stare. "What do you mean?"

"I mean," Travis went on slowly, walking toward the fireplace, "that there wasn't anything there. Just leaves and branches. Nothing else."

"But . . . but that's impossible. I saw it myself. I was right there in the window."

Gayle's voice rose anxiously. Travis stopped beside the hearth and leaned back, resting both elbows on the mantel.

"Tell me what it looked like," he said.

Gayle could still see it, all too horribly in her mind. "It was long—like this." She spaced her hands apart to indicate a length of about sixteen inches. "And at first I thought it was an animal—a squirrel or something. But then I opened the window, and I touched it and—" She broke off, her fists clenching defensively. "I know it was hair, Travis. I could tell by the feel of it. Human hair. And it was red."

Travis's gaze didn't waver. It was calm and dark and penetrating, as though he were studying her beneath a microscope.

"I'm wondering," he said at last, "why you said it was the Stalker."

Gayle deliberately kept her eyes off the rocking chair. "Well . . . I mean . . . don't you know about him?"

"Of course I know about him. Everyone around here knows about him."

"There were some old newspapers in Aunt Pat's house," Gayle said, as though that should explain everything.

Travis gave a slow nod. "I see. So you read these

articles about the Pine Ridge Stalker, and then you went to bed. And then you dreamed about red hair hanging outside your window."

Gayle's chin lifted. "It wasn't a dream."

"How can you be so sure?"

"Trust me. I'm sure."

"You did get a pretty bad bump on the head, you know."

"I know all about the bump on my head, thank you very much."

Travis regarded her thoughtfully. He shifted his lean frame away from the fireplace. "Okay, let's look at our options. Maybe it *was* really an animal. Maybe you dreamed it. Or maybe someone hung it there on purpose."

Gayle drew her breath in sharply. Travis frowned.

"The question is, why would someone do that?" he went on. "You don't live here, and nobody really knows you. You only got here this evening—you haven't even had *time* to be stalked yet."

"Is that supposed to be funny?"

Travis shrugged his shoulders. "I don't hear anyone laughing."

"So what about the hospital?" Gayle reminded him. "What about the man I saw in the window?"

"You know as well as I do, there wasn't anyone in that window. It was a loose brick, that's all."

"Fine. Thanks for taking this so seriously."

Gayle turned on her heel and started for the door, but Travis's voice stopped her cold.

"I do take this seriously. More seriously than you could ever know."

And what was it about his voice that sent a chill

straight through her? That kept her from looking back at his face?

Gayle wasn't sure.

All she knew was that she wanted to get away from him as quickly as possible.

Back to the house . . .

Behind locked doors.

10

Gayle wasn't sure she slept anymore at all.

Tossing and turning, it seemed the night would never end, and when the first hint of daybreak began to lighten the curtains, she got up, dressed, and went downstairs.

The house was even hotter than before. As she came into the kitchen, she heard a door slam, and then a series of thuds and bangings that sent her hurrying out to the porch. To her surprise, Travis was there, a toolbox open beside him. He was squatting down on his heels, examining several small pieces of metal, and one of the air conditioners was propped against the wall at his back.

"This window unit's out again," Travis informed her without bothering to look up. "I'm not sure I can fix it this time."

He'd tied a red bandanna around his forehead to keep his hair back from his face. Somehow it made his tan seem darker and emphasized the blackness of his eyes.

"How'd you get in?" Gayle demanded.

Travis jerked his chin in the direction of the floor. Gayle saw the metal ring lying there, full of keys.

"Well," she said blandly. "I guess it doesn't do me much good to lock the doors."

"Your aunt never did." Travis shrugged. "But now she forgets sometimes. And I like knowing I can get to her fast, if I have to."

"So I guess she depends on you a lot," Gayle offered grudgingly.

Again Travis shrugged, and she walked back into the kitchen.

"I need to check on Stephanie," she mumbled.

"The number's on that list by the phone."

"A lot of help that is. It doesn't even say who the numbers belong to."

"Mine's the first. Hospital's second from the bottom."

"You really do know Aunt Pat's habits, don't you?"

"I made the list."

"Oh." In spite of herself Gayle almost smiled. "Do you want something to eat?"

"Already ate."

"When'd you get up? Before sunrise?"

"Some of us have work to do."

Gayle hadn't realized how hungry she was, but now it occurred to her that she hadn't eaten since yesterday afternoon. *Well, maybe I did imagine that thing in the tree last night. . . . Maybe I was suffering from hunger hallucinations.*

As though reading her mind, Travis asked, "Any more problems last night?"

"No. No problems."

"How's your head?"

"Still on my shoulders."

Gayle thought he might have chuckled at that, but she couldn't be sure. She didn't feel like talking about it anymore—and especially not with him. In the bright light of a new morning it *did* almost seem as if she'd dreamed it—in fact, the whole thing about the Stalker seemed like one bad, fading memory. Today it made perfect sense that a brick had come loose from that building . . . and that what she'd really seen was the backside of some animal up in that maple tree.

Today was a new day.

She'd go visit Stephanie, and Aunt Pat would be coming home, and their summer vacation would carry on just the way they'd planned.

"What happened to the window screens?" she asked him. She pulled the curtains wider over the kitchen sink and gazed out into the already sun-scorched morning.

"Your aunt ordered new ones and had me take the old ones down."

"I wish she'd waited till the new ones came in."

"I tried to tell her that, too," Travis grumbled. "By the way, I fixed your trunk."

"When?"

"Earlier. It should hold all right. At least till you can get it to a body shop."

"Well . . . thanks. I appreciate it."

There was no answering response. Gayle rummaged in the pantry, pulled out some homemade bread and jam, then went to the refrigerator. The shelves were practically empty.

"The quiche," she murmured. Then calling to Travis, "Where's that quiche Aunt Pat made?"

Travis was hammering. She knew he could hear her above the noise, but he kept on hammering anyway. When he finally stopped, there was a brief moment of silence before he answered.

"I got rid of it."

Gayle frowned and turned toward the porch. "You did?"

"You heard what Doc said—it was probably spoiled. I thought you'd want it out of here. Anyway, it'd just remind you of your friend, wouldn't it?"

Gayle felt a twinge of guilt. She closed the refrigerator door and picked up the phone. At the hospital a nurse informed her that Stephanie had been moved to a room and was sleeping. When she suggested Gayle call back later, Gayle hung up and stared at the floor.

"So how is she?"

Gayle nearly jumped out of her skin. She hadn't heard Travis come up behind her, and he was so close she could have touched him. She turned and backed up against the sink.

"Sleeping. But I'd like to go see her today."

"You can ride in with me, if you want. I have to go into town for parts."

She hesitated, then managed a halfhearted smile. "Okay. Thanks."

"And you should get out of here, if you want to stay cool. It'll be miserable in this house by noon."

"I'll go out on the front porch. I brought books to read."

"There's always the pond," Travis suggested. "I won't be leaving for a couple hours."

He turned and started to walk away, when another thought came to Gayle's mind.

"Did you tell the sheriff what Steph and I found yesterday?" she reminded him. "At the garbage dump?"

Travis stopped, his arms at his sides. His long fingers clenched slowly into fists . . . straightened again. He kept his back to her.

"He's checking on it," Travis said.

Gayle watched as he returned to his work. Then she smeared strawberry jam between two slices of bread and took her sandwich with her out the front door.

Four more cats greeted her on the porch. They were lounging all over the porch swing, and Gayle gave each of them a polite pat before she went down the steps and wandered back along the side of the house.

She didn't feel like reading. She stood for a long while beneath her bedroom window, gazing up through the branches of the old maple tree. The thing was so huge, it'd be easy for someone to climb up there and hang something from one of the limbs. After finishing off her breakfast, Gayle wiped her hands on her shorts and put one foot up on the bottom branch. In no time at all she'd managed to climb the distance, and then she perched there, squinting in through the open curtains of her room.

She began searching through the leaves, looking for any clue as to what she'd seen there last night. But though she found bugs and spiderwebs and part of an abandoned bird's nest, there wasn't any sign of long, red hair.

Discouraged, Gayle climbed down again. *This is too weird. . . . Maybe my imagination is going crazy on me. . . . Maybe I needed a vacation more than I thought.*

She kept on walking, heading off behind the house. She could see the barn, slightly downhill and far to the left, with the fenced barnyard around it, and the chicken house sitting even lower down the slope. Travis's cabin looked even smaller and dingier now in daylight. It was sturdy enough, Gayle didn't doubt that, but she wondered why Aunt Pat had never had it painted.

She continued up the gentle rise of the hill, toward the pasture that was bordered on two sides by thick woods. Cows gazed at her calmly as she walked past; none of them seemed the least concerned with her presence. She turned into the woods and followed the well-worn path, wondering if anything had changed.

She needn't have worried—the pond was every bit as beautiful as she remembered it. The water spread calm and deep beneath shady trees, fed by a creek that trickled down from the bluff overhead. Gayle picked her way carefully through the weeds to the edge of the pond. It was dark here and cool and very quiet. When they were little, she and her brothers used to swim for hours and hours, pretending to be pirates and dolphins and magical sea creatures. . . .

Gayle smiled at the memory. She slipped off her shoes and sat down on the shore, easing her feet into the water. She gasped at the first icy shock of it

over her toes. She caught the silvery flash of a fin
. . . heard the startled plop of a frog as it leaped
from the weeds into the water.

She wished Stephanie were here to share this
with her now. She wished Aunt Pat would get
home.

She leaned back in the grass, resting her head on
folded arms. Tiny patches of sunlight wavered
through the leaves overhead, and she closed her
eyes against its speckly brightness. She was surprised that she felt so relaxed . . . so sleepy. After
all, she'd only been up a little while. . . .

Her mind began to drift. She knew she should
make herself get up and go back to the house. She
had to go see Stephanie . . . make sure Stephanie
was okay . . . but it felt so nice lying here in the
tall, cool grass. . . .

From some realm of consciousness she knew
she was dozing off. She managed to roll over onto
her stomach, but couldn't muster the strength to
stay awake. She could hear cows lowing in the distance . . . a dog barking far away . . . the sharp
snap of a twig . . .

Groggily she lifted her head.

She glanced behind her at the shoreline but saw
nothing. She peered through the tall blades of grass
toward the woods, and as her eyes swept over one
particular spot, she caught a glimpse of red flashing
though the green of the trees. *A shirt? A cap?*

Slowly she drew in her breath. Something fluttered overhead, and she glanced up, just in time to
see a bright red cardinal eyeing her from its branch.

"Oh"—she sighed—"it's just you."

Feeling foolish, she lowered her head back to her

arms and closed her eyes in relief. How stupid could she be—who'd be out here spying on her anyway?

*Quit being so jumpy. Just lie here for five more minutes. Then you've **got** to get up and go to town.*

She smiled lazily to herself. The sounds and smells of summer wafted over her, lulling her back to a doze.

There was no warning.

No warning at all.

Only instant terror as she felt herself being forced onto her back and pinned to the ground.

11

Gayle shrieked and struggled, kicking out wildly with her legs. There was a loud cry of pain, and as a shadowy figure toppled backward into the grass, Gayle jumped to her feet. She looked around for a weapon, grabbed the first thing she saw, then took one wide swing with a broken tree branch.

"Okay! Okay! I give up!"

Gayle realized she was standing over her attacker now, the branch aimed at his head. He didn't look half as scary as she'd thought he would—in fact, he looked almost helpless, his body curled defensively, his arms crossed over his face. As her fear began to ebb, she relaxed her grip a little and took a cautious step back.

"Did you hear me?" the voice tried again. "I said—"

"I heard you," Gayle said angrily. "What the hell do you think you're doing!"

For a minute he didn't speak. Then his voice came again, tentatively. "Begging for my life?"

Gayle stared at him. One of his arms moved a little, and she saw blue eyes peering out at her from beneath it. She lifted the branch again, hesitated, then slowly lowered it to the ground.

"Get up," she said at last.

"Why?" He didn't move. "So you can knock me down again? No, thanks."

His arm shifted a little more. Gayle could see most of his head now, his tousled sun-bleached hair, and those blue, blue eyes still watching her guardedly.

"Well," he said at last, "at least I'm glad you're not dead."

"Dead!" Gayle's mouth opened in surprise. She thought of the hair hanging outside her window . . . her accident at the hospital. "What do you mean? Why would I be dead!"

The young man cocked his head. He leaned back, propping himself up on his elbows. His cutoffs were ripped and stained; there were wide streaks of dirt across his bare chest. "Well, you were lying facedown in the weeds, and you weren't moving— what *else* was I supposed to think?"

"Who are you?"

"Doug Wilson. Who are *you?*"

"Never mind who I am. Get up and stand over there."

"Over where? Is this what I get for trying to be a good samaritan?"

"You scared the life out of me."

"Well, you nearly scared something else out of me. So we're even."

Gayle's grip tightened again on her branch. Doug

Wilson got up slowly, backed off, then watched as she put her weapon down. He looked very relieved.

"Don't you know better than to sneak up on people like that?" Gayle accused him.

"Sorry. But I don't usually find people lying around looking like they're dead."

"What are you doing here? This is private property."

"Oh, I get it. Then you must be Pat's niece."

"How'd you know that?"

"We're neighbors. My family rents pastureland from your aunt. We keep some of our horses at her barn, too."

Gayle stared at him suspiciously, but now he was looking amused.

"Well," she said, with all the dignity she could manage. "I didn't know."

"Is that the closest I'm going to get to an apology?"

Gayle started to snap back at him, but the words caught in her throat. He had a teasing sort of grin, and his eyes crinkled up when he smiled. She couldn't help smiling back.

"Sorry," she mumbled.

"Accepted. But humor me here—you really are okay?"

"Yes, I'm fine. I dozed off, is all. How'd you even find me?"

"I came to do some fishing. Never expected to see you, though. When'd you get in?"

"Yesterday. Last night, really."

"You're pretty damn strong," he said good-naturedly, brushing himself off. He leaned over, retrieved a red cap from the weeds, and clamped it firmly on his head. "I think you broke some of my ribs."

"Really?"

"No." His grin widened. "You like to fish?"

"I used to fish," Gayle admitted. "Aunt Pat and I used to come down here early in the mornings—"

"Care to join me?"

"Well . . .the thing is, I have these things I really have to do—"

"I've heard *much* more original excuses than that."

"No, seriously," Gayle insisted. "My friend's in the hospital, and Travis is taking me to town and—"

"Hold it." Doug held up both hands and shook his head. "Start from the beginning. What friend? And what about the hospital? I thought you said you just got here last night."

Gayle sighed. "It's a long story."

"I'm a good listener."

"Well . . ."

"It's not like we're total strangers, you know. Your aunt's told me all about you. As a matter of fact, she tried to bribe me into asking you out while you were here."

Gayle's cheeks reddened. "Oh, no . . . she didn't really, did she?"

That grin again. God, he was really cute, Gayle thought. Self-assured like Travis but without that hard, cynical edge . .

Doug gave her a wink. "I told her she might have to bribe *you* to accept."

"This is so embarrassing. I'm really sorry—"

"I'm not." Doug grinned again and walked toward the shore. As Gayle watched, he gathered a fishing rod and an old rusted coffee can.

"Sure you don't want to join me?" he asked again, but Gayle shook her head.

"No. Thanks a lot, but really, I need to go. My friend—"

"The one in the hospital?"

"Right. She got food poisoning last night, and see, she accidentally fell on this knife—"

Doug's eyes widened. "Is she all right?"

"Yes, she's fine—at least, I think she is. That's why I'm going to the hospital to check on her. If it hadn't been for Travis, she might have died. But when I walked in, he was there with her; he'd found her on the kitchen floor—"

"Travis did?"

Gayle nodded. "Really, he saved her life."

"That must have been pretty upsetting for Travis," Doug reflected.

"Well, I guess so, but he seemed pretty calm about it."

"No, I mean, after what happened with his girlfriend and all, seeing your friend in trouble like that."

"What about his girlfriend?"

"Oh. Your aunt didn't tell you?"

Gayle shook her head.

"She disappeared," Doug said quietly. "No trace, no clues, no nothing."

Gayle's cheeks weren't flushed now. She could feel the color draining out of them.

"Travis was a major suspect for a while, but they never could prove anything." Doug paused and shook his head. "Your aunt was the only one who'd hire him."

12

The lovely summer morning seemed to darken.

Gayle looked up through the trees, thinking the sky must have clouded over—but when she saw the sun still shimmering beyond the leaves, she realized the darkness was only in her mind.

"Why . . . why was he a suspect?" she mumbled.

Doug eased down on the embankment. He pulled a long, fat worm from the coffee can and calmly proceeded to bait his hook.

"Seems her brother heard them having one hell of an argument the night before she disappeared," he explained. "Travis was really mad—threatening her, in fact."

"But why?"

"I guess she'd decided to break up with him—and he wasn't being very cooperative about it." Doug glanced up at her. A shock of white-blond hair fell into his eyes, and he swiped it impatiently with the back of one hand. "So when she suddenly vanished off the face of the earth . . ."

He left the sentence unfinished. Gayle eased down beside him in the grass. She remembered the scene at the hospital last night—how everyone had stared at Travis and acted so strange . . . what Dr. Maxwell had said about having to report anything suspicious . . .

"So . . . does everyone else think Travis is guilty?" she finally asked.

Doug seemed to be weighing her question. He cast his line into the water, then gazed calmly across the surface of the pond.

"Nobody really knows anything about Travis," he said quietly. "But right after he moved to Pine Ridge . . . bad things started happening."

"What kinds of things?" Gayle asked, though deep in her heart she already knew what Doug was going to say.

Doug reeled in his line a few inches. "You've heard of the Pine Ridge Stalker?" Seeing Gayle's nod, his voice lowered solemnly. "Not long after Travis showed up in town, that's when the first girl disappeared."

"But . . . people always suspect outsiders, don't they? That doesn't mean they're guilty."

"No . . . but it doesn't help when you're a loner like Travis. When you don't even try to make friends—when you won't have much to do with the folks who live here. Let's just say he hasn't done a lot to make himself likable."

"But if he knows everybody's watching him, then why would he do something to his own girlfriend? That's so obvious. So *stupid.*"

"Look, I'm not saying he's innocent or guilty. All I'm saying is what I've heard."

Gayle watched his fishing rod dangling out over the water. She watched as he tipped back the brim of his cap.

"Is that the last girl who disappeared? His girlfriend?"

Doug nodded. "Yep. And she had long pretty red hair." His eyes flicked briefly to her face. "Like you."

Long red hair . . . long red hair hanging from the tree outside my window . . . long red hair that I touched—that I dreamed—that I only imagined—

"What else?" she heard herself say.

"What else what?"

"His girlfriend," Gayle said quickly. She didn't know why she'd said that; she wasn't thinking—it had just burst out. "What did she look like? Was she nice?"

"Yeah, I guess." Doug's brow furrowed in thought. "She used to come into my brother-in-law's place—I'd see her when I was working there. She was *very* pretty. Always had a smile."

Gayle's emotions felt open and raw. She nodded at him to continue, then leaned back, fixing her eyes on the canopy of leaves overhead.

"Her family took it really hard. Her mom had a nervous breakdown and had to leave town for a while. And old man Gentry's offering one hell of a reward for any information about—"

Gayle sat up again in surprise. "What's their last name?"

"Gentry. Why?"

"I met a guy at the hospital last night—*his* name was Gentry."

"Right," Doug said. "Mark Gentry. He's got a

summer job there, works as an orderly. Nancy—Travis's girlfriend—she was Mark's sister."

"So that's why he seemed to hate Travis so much," Gayle murmured, and Doug threw her a curious look.

"Yeah, he hates Travis, all right. He totally believes Travis killed her."

The sandwich Gayle had eaten did a flip-flop in her stomach. She could still see the way Mark Gentry had looked at Travis the night before. And she could still hear those words Mark Gentry had spoken to her—*"You should think about keeping better company."*

And "How come Travis wasn't with you?" he'd asked her. "Where was Travis?" he'd asked her—after she'd gotten hit on the head by that loose brick . . . after those birds had flown up . . . *after I saw that shadow at the window. . . .*

"—when Travis wouldn't give it back," Doug was saying, and Gayle snapped back to the present.

"Sorry," she mumbled. "What'd you say?"

"I said Mark hated him even more when Travis wouldn't give it back." Seeing Gayle's blank expression, Doug sighed and backtracked once again. "Mark had given Nancy a ring for her birthday, and he told Travis he wanted it back. Sentimental value, he said, nothing Travis would want to keep anyway. But Travis said he didn't know anything about the ring. He swore up and down he didn't have it."

"What do *you* think?" Gayle asked.

"Well, I know what *Mark* thinks. Mark thinks Travis lied—that he kept the ring and pawned it to get cash. Mark even threatened to break into

Travis's place. Said he'd tear it apart till he found that ring."

Ring . . .

Something was nagging at the back of Gayle's mind. Something familiar . . . familiar and awful . . .

"A birthday ring," she murmured, frowning. "That's so sad."

And *"I can't make it out," Stephanie had said. "I think it might be a flower. . . ."*

"She loved flowers." Doug smiled. "Mark had given her the ring for her eighteenth birthday. Little silver ring . . ."

And *"does it look like a rose . . ." Stephanie had said. . . .*

Doug sighed. "Silver. With a rose in the middle."

Oh, no. . . . Oh, please, no. . . .

"Gayle?" Doug asked, his voice full of concern. "Hey . . . are you all right?"

But Gayle was covering her face with her hands. Trying to shut out the sight of that blackened arm . . . that charred ring . . . the ring with the rose in the middle.

13

"Gayle?" he asked again, but as Gayle lowered her hands and looked up, she let out a startled gasp.

She hadn't heard anyone approaching.

But now, as she stared wide-eyed past Doug, she could see Travis standing at the edge of the trees, watching them. How long had he been there? How much of their conversation had he heard? But Travis's expression gave nothing away, and as he stepped closer, Doug turned in surprise.

Doug's eyes went swiftly from Travis's face back to Gayle's. She could tell he was wondering the same things, but he merely lifted one hand in a casual wave and focused his attention back to his fishing rod.

"Hey, Travis. Looking for a place to stay cool?"

Travis walked up beside them. He acknowledged Doug with a curt nod, but spoke directly to Gayle. "I'm leaving, if you want a ride."

"Now?" She jumped up, brushing grass from her shorts. "I thought it'd be—"

"Changed my mind." Travis turned back toward the path. "Thought I had what I needed, but I don't."

"Okay, I'm coming."

She could still see the concern in Doug's eyes, but Gayle merely threw him a quick smile.

"Nice to meet you. And thanks."

"No problem. Hey, will I be seeing you again?"

"Oh. Well . . . I hope so."

"Even without a bribe?"

"Even without a bribe," she promised.

Doug grinned and waved, and Gayle followed Travis back to the house.

She felt awkward riding into town with him. Awkward and morbidly curious, now that Doug had told her about Nancy Gentry. She didn't feel like talking—she kept going over and over Doug's conversation in her mind—but if Travis even took note of her silence, it didn't seem to bother him. He kept his eyes on the road and didn't speak.

Why didn't you tell Doug about the arm—about the ring!

Gayle rubbed a hand over her eyes, trying to block out the grisly scene at the garbage dump. A silver ring with a rose in the middle! *But I can't be a hundred percent sure that's what Stephanie saw, can I?—and I didn't actually see it clearly myself, did I? It could be just some weird coincidence. . . .*

She gave an inward groan. She *should* have told Doug—why hadn't she? *Because I don't really know him—because Travis already told the sheriff about it, and it's just better to let the authorities handle it, better not to get involved. We just came here to have a good time, not to get wrapped up in some murder—*

Murder . . .

Travis's girlfriend . . . murdered? Like all those other girls with red hair? But it was speculation, really—no one could *prove* they'd been killed—after all, every one of them had vanished without a trace. . . .

And Travis was a suspect.

Gayle glanced over at his rugged profile. He still wore the red bandanna around his forehead, and the breeze from the open window whipped the sides of his hair about his handsome face. Travis couldn't be a murderer. He'd *helped* them last night—he'd *saved* Stephanie's life. . . .

Or had he?

Gayle kept her eyes on him and frowned. How could she really be sure she hadn't interrupted something gruesome and horrible when she'd come into the kitchen—how could she be sure Travis hadn't lied to her? If she hadn't come into the kitchen when she did, would Stephanie be missing by now—vanished without a single clue?

But of course she wouldn't be missing, Gayle told herself furiously—*Stephanie doesn't have red hair. Are you crazy? What are you thinking!*

And yet the truth was, she *couldn't* be sure. Not really. With Stephanie lying there on the floor and Travis bending over her with a knife, she couldn't be sure of *anything,* not anything at all.

She realized she was still staring at Travis and quickly averted her gaze.

"Doug seems nice," she said, just for the sake of conversation. "Do you know him?"

"I see him around."

"How long has his family been renting from Aunt Pat?"

"About six months." He threw her a sharp glance. "Why?"

"No reason. I just wondered." She tried to keep her voice casual. "So . . . does he work on their farm?"

"Sometimes. Mostly he works for his brother-in-law. The guy has a meat market over in Braxley."

Gayle's eyes widened. "A meat market?"

"He's a butcher. Didn't Doug tell you?"

"No," Gayle said quickly. "He didn't say anything about that."

Travis's eyes slid smoothly to her face. "I'm surprised. You two seemed to be so deep in conversation."

Gayle felt flushed. She deliberately turned toward her window. "Just small talk. Nothing, really. You know . . . just getting acquainted."

"If you say so."

Something about the way Travis said that . . . Gayle suppressed a shudder and lapsed into silence. *So maybe he did hear us, after all. . . .* She didn't know why she felt so guilty about it. She wished he'd drive faster so she could get out of the truck.

"Oh, by the way," Travis said casually. "The sheriff called while you were gone. Said he couldn't find a thing out at that roadside stand of yours."

Gayle felt as if she'd been slapped. She hesitated, trying to keep her voice calm. "Nothing? Are you sure? Nothing in the dump?"

"That's what he said. But you could have been mistaken, right?"

Gayle nodded miserably. "Well," she choked, "it was really getting dark by then—"

"So you probably didn't get a real good look at it," Travis finished for her.

Gayle nodded slowly. "Probably not."

"Things look different at twilight." He sounded so matter of fact. "People think they see all sorts of things they don't really see."

"Right," Gayle said mechanically. "I mean, it could have been anything. . . ." *But it wasn't. . . . It was an arm. . . . And there was a hand . . . and the hand had a ring. . . .*

"Maybe even a tree branch," he said.

"They never could prove anything. . . . Your aunt was the only one who'd hire him. . . ."

"Yes," Gayle murmured. "Even that."

"Well," Travis said. "We're here."

Gayle felt the truck turning, saw the hospital ahead. Travis pulled up to the main entrance this time and waited while she got out.

"I'll be back in about forty-five minutes," he told her.

Gayle nodded and walked into the building. She felt like a robot. Her mind felt as if it were going to burst.

I have to go back to that garbage dump.

She stopped in surprise—put a hand out to the wall.

I have to go back there and look for myself.

It couldn't be true—someone was lying— someone *had* to be lying. She'd seen the arm with

111

her own eyes, and Stephanie'd seen it, too. They'd both stood there looking at it until that strange bright light had hit them in the eyes—

That light . . .

Maybe it *had* been someone with a flashlight. And maybe that someone had seen the arm, too.

Gayle made herself walk to the elevators. She pressed the button, then leaned her forehead against the wall. Did the person with the flashlight see the arm? Or did he *put* it there?

Gayle's heart clenched in her chest. Whoever it was *must* have gotten a good look at the two of them—after all, she and Stephanie had been blinded and paralyzed by that bright light. *Just like deer on a highway right before a car cuts them down. . . .*

Gayle fought down a wave of panic. No, she wouldn't jump to conclusions, at least not yet. She'd talk to Stephanie about it first. Steph would have good ideas—they'd talk it over and figure out what to do.

But the minute she laid eyes on Stephanie, Gayle decided not to say a word. She'd never seen her friend look so awful. Stephanie was awake, but groggy—pale and wan and so weak she could hardly talk. There was an IV running into one arm, and Gayle made a stoic effort to hide her alarm.

"Hey, stranger," Gayle said softly. She gave her friend a cautious hug, but Stephanie winced just the same.

"Some vacation," Stephanie murmured. "Next time remind me to stay home."

Gayle eased down on the edge of the bed.

"Steph," she said, smoothing her friend's hair back from her face, "what happened? Do you remember anything?"

For a minute she thought Stephanie wasn't going to answer. Then slowly her friend mumbled, "I remember feeling really sick . . . worst cramps in my life. I felt like I was going to throw up. Next thing I know . . . I'm falling. And then . . . I woke up here."

Gayle peered urgently into Stephanie's bleary eyes. "You didn't see anyone come into the kitchen? You didn't hear anything?"

Steph paused, looking puzzled. "Should I have?"

Relieved, Gayle shook her head. "You remember that guy whose truck we hit—"

"The one without headlights?"

"That's the one. His name is Travis and guess what? He's Aunt Pat's handyman. And last night he saved your life."

"How?" Steph made an attempt to shake her head. "I don't remember."

"You were holding a knife, do you remember that? And you fell on it. He found you on the floor and rushed you to the emergency room."

"What knife?" Stephanie murmured. "What knife was I holding?"

Gayle stared down at the ghostly face, trying to keep her voice calm. "Steph . . . *were* you holding a knife? Try to think. Try to remember."

Stephanie closed her eyes. She let out a long, ragged sigh.

"I . . . might have been. I took a bite first . . . with my fingers. Then another one . . . maybe more, I don't know. Then I think . . . I remember opening the kitchen drawer . . . starting to feel sick. I was going to cut a slice . . . put it on a plate . . . but . . ." She turned her head restlessly. "I don't remember if I found a knife . . . I was just so sick. So maybe I did find it. I can't remember."

Gayle nodded slowly. She wanted to tell Stephanie about the Stalker, about her own mishap at the hospital last night, about the hair hanging outside her window, about the scrapbook with the clippings, about Doug and Mark and everyone being so suspicious of Travis. . . .

She jumped as Stephanie tried to squeeze her hand. "I ruined our vacation, huh?" Stephanie whispered.

"Don't you dare think that." Gayle hugged her again. "Just get better."

"Bet your aunt thinks I'm so rude."

"She's not even home yet. Travis said she went to some auctions over in some little town around here, but she's coming back today."

To Gayle's surprise Stephanie frowned. "Then why'd she leave that note?"

"Travis said *he* wrote it."

"You . . . believe him?"

Gayle forced cheerfulness into her voice. "Why shouldn't I believe him? He seems like a really nice guy."

Stephanie groaned. "Take me home, Gayle. I don't like it here."

"You'll be okay. The doctor said—"

"I kept waking up all night," Stephanie interrupted. "I kept waking up, I kept thinking someone was here in my room. I was all groggy, and I couldn't lift my head . . . so scared . . . but when I'd try and look, the room was always empty."

Gayle patted her friend's shoulder. She could feel that strange coldness again, squeezing around her own heart, but she made herself smile down at Stephanie.

"Weird dreams, Steph. Probably from the medicine they're giving you."

"I guess." Stephanie sighed. "I guess you're right." She closed her eyes and turned her head away. "I guess . . . you're right."

Gayle waited for Stephanie's breathing to grow deep and regular, then she went out to speak with the nurse. The doctor wouldn't be in till later, she was told, and the lab results hadn't come back yet. The hospital had left a message on Stephanie's parents' machine. *Thank God they're gone.*

Gayle headed down to the lobby, unable to shake her growing sense of unease. She didn't know what she'd expected, exactly. After all, Stephanie *did* have a knife wound. . . . She *had* been through a terrible ordeal. . . .

Still, Gayle hadn't been prepared for how bad her friend looked. And as she got off the elevator, still thinking about Stephanie, she was startled to hear a shout and then feel something bump against her side. Jerking around in surprise, she saw the gurney she'd collided with, and the familiar face that was pushing it.

"Hop on. I'll give you the ride of your life."

As Gayle stared at him, Mark Gentry gave her an irresistible smile, nodding at the empty cart.

"I'm just on my way to the morgue," he added. "Care to join me?"

Gayle suppressed a shudder and leveled her gaze to meet his. "No, thanks."

"Where's your boyfriend?" Mark asked casually.

"I don't have a boyfriend. So I can't imagine who you're talking about."

"Oh, I bet you can."

Gayle's voice was stiff. "He *did* save my friend's life, you know."

"Ah, yes. And how gallant of him."

Gayle ignored his sarcasm. She turned away, but Mark fell into step beside her, pushing the gurney as they walked.

"But maybe you don't know the truth about him," Mark went on, his tone hard beneath all the pleasantry. "For instance . . . did you know you're staying out there all alone with a genuine magician?"

Gayle shot him an annoyed glance. She wished he'd go away. "Magician?"

"Yeah. He makes girls disappear."

"That's not even funny," she retorted. "And I *do* know about the Stalker, and I think you're rude."

Mark chuckled at that. "Even though I'm right?"

That scrapbook in the cabin . . . "Your aunt was the only one who'd hire him. . . ."

"You're pretty sure of yourself, aren't you?" Gayle said quickly. She tried to shut her mind, tried to block out those dark suspicions of Travis, tried to concentrate on what Mark was saying.

"I know trash when I see it. And Travis McGraw is trash, pure and simple—"

"I have to go," Gayle interrupted. She stopped,

but Mark stopped, too, blocking the doorway. "Please let me by."

"Where are you going?"

"That's none of your business."

She turned in another direction, but he gave the gurney a shove, blocking that escape route as well. Gayle spun around to face him. She clenched her arms over her chest and glared.

"Get out of my way," she said angrily.

Mark seemed to be considering this. He reached over and, to Gayle's annoyance, lightly touched one of her earrings.

"Nice," he approved. "Sort of matches your hair."

"Get out of my way *now.*"

"Only if you'll go out with me."

"Go *out* with you?" Gayle backed away from him. "You must be crazy."

"Hey, you might get to like me if you knew me better."

"I know you as well as I want to know you. And believe me, it's *not going* to get any better."

Mark gave that slow, self-assured smile. "You're good," he said, impressed. "But you must have some real doubts about what happened to your friend. *And* about that accident you had here last night. In fact, if I were you, I couldn't *wait* to talk to me. Just to satisfy my own curiosity."

Gayle felt herself weakening. She gazed into his eyes, then shook her head firmly. "No."

"Hey, I rescued you last night." Mark spread his hands in a gesture of supplication. "How bad could I be?"

"Is that a rhetorical question?"

"Look, I'm going on break right now. Give me fifteen minutes. Let me prove to you I'm not such a bad guy."

"It'd take a lot more than fifteen minutes to do that."

"Hmmm. Is that a proposition?"

In spite of her annoyance Gayle gave in to a smile. "Okay." She sighed. "But just for—"

Without warning, Mark's expression changed. Gayle saw the cockiness melt into a scowl, and she suddenly realized he was looking at something behind her. Turning around, she saw Travis walking into the lobby, and at the same instant Mark gave the gurney a push.

"I'll pick you up later," he said quickly.

"You'll—what?"

"Seven o'clock. We'll go someplace we can talk."

And as Gayle stared after him, he vanished down the hallway without so much as a backward glance.

14

She was relieved to get home again.

As before, Travis barely spoke to her, but this time she found herself wondering if it had something to do with Mark Gentry. She wished Travis hadn't seen her talking to Mark—on the other hand, it made her mad that she was even worrying about it. It wasn't any of Travis's business *who* she talked to, she reminded herself. And what a stupid situation to get into, anyway! She couldn't believe she'd agreed to meet Mark tonight. She didn't even know him—and she certainly had no desire to get mixed up in anything more than she already was.

She jumped from the truck the minute they stopped, then hurried into the house. Aunt Pat wasn't back yet. Gayle could tell immediately that her aunt hadn't arrived, and she felt more uneasy than ever. This was supposed to be her vacation—she was tired of feeling worried and scared about everything.

"Can't you get that stupid air conditioner fixed?"

she complained to Travis as he resumed his work on the back porch. "It's like a desert in here!"

Travis didn't answer. His silence only made her angrier.

"As if I need one more problem in my life," she muttered, pouring herself a glass of ice water from the refrigerator.

She didn't think Travis had heard, but when she turned around, he was staring at her with a frown as irritable as her own. Gayle stared back at him, Mark Gentry's accusations pounding through her head—*"He makes girls disappear . . . disappear . . . disappear . . ."* She saw Travis's eyes narrow, she saw his lips press into a thin, hard line—and for a split second she felt a rush of panic, as though he could see right inside her thoughts.

Abruptly Gayle turned her back on him. Mark was wrong about Travis—he *had* to be. And how must Travis feel, she wondered, losing Nancy and then being blamed for her disappearance? Gayle couldn't even imagine.

She went deliberately around the kitchen, slamming cabinet doors and looking for something to eat. Then she started on the kitchen drawers, opening and closing them all along the length of the counter. Finally she looked back at Travis, but his attention was on the air conditioner. She made herself a cheese sandwich and took it outside.

There was a hammock in the side yard, strung beneath the maples and elms along the edge of the woods. It looked so inviting, so cool beneath the shady boughs, that Gayle decided to eat her lunch there.

She climbed in and lay back, munching slowly on her sandwich, staring up at the patterns of sunlight and shade. Nothing was going right, nothing was like it was supposed to be, and now here it was— morning gone and afternoon creeping by—and still no Aunt Pat. She finished eating and let her eyelids droop shut. Except for some bees in the flowerbeds near the house, there was no sound out here at all.

Can't go to sleep . . . have to think . . .

It was silly, she knew, but she couldn't shake that nagging uneasiness that had plagued her all day. She opened her eyes and raised up a little, looking nervously off through the trees. *Weird . . .* For a split second it almost looked as if someone was standing there—a dark shape just slightly different from the rest of the shadows—hovering just inside the thickness of the woods. Gayle lifted her head higher, then frowned. The shape wasn't there now—maybe it hadn't really been there at all. Puzzled, she climbed out of the hammock and started walking toward the end of the yard.

Halfway there, she stopped. She could feel the hairs lifting along the back of her neck; she could feel her heart beginning to quicken. *Go on—what's the matter with you?* And yet she *couldn't* go on— she couldn't even move one foot in front of the other. Suddenly she was filled with such a terrible sense of danger that all she could do was stand there staring helplessly into the fathomless shadows of the woods.

Go on . . . don't be so silly. . . .

She glanced back over her shoulder at the house.

She wrapped her arms tightly around her chest, and she felt her heart fluttering wildly in her throat. *I can't—I can't! Something's in there!*

Gayle wanted to run. Suddenly, more than anything else in the world, she wanted to turn and run as fast and as far as she could. She was paralyzed—frozen beneath a horrible gaze she couldn't even see—yet she *knew* it was there, rooting her to the spot—

She knew someone was there.

Watching.

Her ears strained through the silence. For a split second she thought she heard a twig snap, the whisper of leaves rustling and—and *what? Footsteps? Footsteps sneaking? Hurrying away?*

She tried to yell. She tried to yell for Travis, but nothing would come out. Her heart echoed loudly in her ears. She could feel the sweat running from her forehead. *Somebody help me—somebody, please . . .*

And then it was gone.

Just as quickly as she'd felt the icy terror, she knew without a doubt the danger was gone, far from her now. Weak and shaky, she finally turned around and stumbled back toward the house. She could hear the sound of an engine from the driveway. She could see the truck backing down toward the road. As in a dream, Gayle started running for the truck, but it kept backing farther and farther away, and she couldn't catch up, she couldn't make him hear—

"Travis! Travis, wait!"

Helplessly she stood there and watched the truck disappear.

The dust settled thickly into the driveway, and silence settled thickly around the house.

I can't stay here. . . . I can't. . . .

She didn't even realize what she was planning to do until she was already doing it. She ran into the house, grabbed her purse, and got into her car. She wasn't sure she'd ever be able to find that roadside stand again, but she was sure going to try.

After several wrong turns, Gayle finally managed to get her bearings and headed down the two-lane road away from town. Thinking back, it didn't seem as if they'd traveled more than twenty minutes from where they'd stopped yesterday until they'd reached Aunt Pat's house. But then again, they'd been scared and upset—and things always seemed so different in the dark. . . .

It was surprisingly easy to find. To Gayle's relief, the roadside stand came into view not long afterward, and she pulled off onto the wide shoulder.

"You really are crazy, you know that," she muttered to herself. "You really are out of your mind."

She sat there for several minutes. Then, steeling herself, she got out, located the pathway, and followed it back through the weeds.

Things *did* look different in daylight. Still dirty and overgrown and abandoned, but somehow not nearly as scary as before. It didn't take her as long to find the garbage dump this time. She stood in the very same spot on the edge of the hollow, and she looked down just as she had the night before.

The mattress was there. The rusted cans and broken bottles and blackened heaps of trash just as before. But the bag—and the arm—were gone.

Gayle felt a knot twisting deep in her stomach.

No arm . . . no fingers . . . definitely no ring.

But I didn't imagine it—I know I didn't—Stephanie saw it, too—we couldn't have both made it up, no matter how scared we were, no matter how dark it was getting. . . .

After a wary glance around, Gayle worked her way down the incline into the dump. She reached out her hand and cautiously lifted one corner of the mattress. Filthy rags . . . smashed boxes . . . a pair of old shoes . . .

No arm.

She thought about that sudden bright light that had blinded them. The person with the flashlight who'd seen their faces—the person they *hadn't* been able to see.

Had she and Stephanie come face to face with the Stalker?

Just the thought sent icy shivers up her spine. She started to leave, then on impulse knelt down and ran her fingers carefully through a mound of ashes. Maybe the ring had fallen off—maybe it was still here somewhere.

She sifted through several more piles, her frustration growing. *Damn!* She should have called someone sooner—should have *made* that woman listen to her. Even if none of this had anything to do with the Stalker, she shouldn't have put it off, she should have been more responsible. She wondered now what Travis had told the sheriff. No one had called her about it, no one had stopped by the house to talk with her, Gayle realized, so maybe he hadn't even mentioned her or Stephanie at all. In fact, maybe it was a *fake* arm, just like Stephanie had suggested—maybe the whole *thing* had been a fake, just some stupid trick to scare people who came to burn their trash.

Gayle almost laughed. Suddenly, more than anything, she wanted to laugh and pretend it had all been some crazy prank. She wanted to laugh about it, and she wanted to get out of here. Now. Right now. *Murders . . . stalkers . . . bodies hidden in trash piles . . .* She couldn't think about any of it anymore, and if she didn't get out of here right now, she was afraid she'd start screaming.

She was wet with sweat, black with dirt and ashes. Her bare legs burned from chiggers and mosquito bites. Miserably she climbed out of the garbage dump and headed back again toward the road.

She saw the broken-down stand. She breathed a sigh of relief and ran for her car.

But the spot where she'd parked was empty.

Her car was gone.

15

Gayle stood there, staring.

She stared and stared at the spot where her car had been, and she felt a crazy urge to laugh and cry at the same time. *This can't be happening to me. I don't believe it.*

Was this the right place? Had she made a mistake—parked somewhere else?

Gayle chewed thoughtfully on her fingernail. Maybe—somehow—the car had rolled out onto the road. Maybe if she started running and looked hard enough, she'd find the stupid thing, still rolling merrily along.

She stepped out onto the road. She could see quite a distance in both directions, far enough to see that it was deserted. She walked back to the shoulder. She looked down at the tire tracks in the dust where the car had swerved onto the blacktop and left without her.

Just my luck. Out here where people don't even

126

lock their doors, and I leave my keys in the car, and someone steals it. Just my stupid luck.

What was she going to do now? Stranded out here like this—it'd take her forever to walk back to Aunt Pat's.

"Damn!"

She picked up a rock and threw it as hard as she could. Weren't things bad enough already? What else could possibly happen on this stupid vacation?

Moaning loudly, Gayle resigned herself to the long trek home. She wiped one arm across her forehead, then set off determinedly down the road.

She barely glanced up as the car went by. She didn't pay attention to it, and she didn't expect the squeal of tires as it stopped several yards past her. She only really noticed when it started backing up again, veering straight toward her.

Gayle froze. In slow motion she saw the car bearing down on her, and she tried to move but couldn't. Fear rose inside her, cold and sick. She felt her feet stumbling backward—she saw the car only inches away—

"Hey! Gayle!"

The car slammed on its brakes. A head appeared out the window, and Doug Wilson yelled again.

"Hey, Gayle! What are you doing out here?"

"Doug!" Gayle burst out. "Thank God—".

"What's going on?" he demanded, glancing first at her, and then at both sides of the road. "How'd you get way out here? Did you walk?"

He looked so totally bewildered that if Gayle hadn't been so upset, she would have laughed.

"Someone stole my car," she told him, fighting back tears instead.

"Your car? When? *Where?*"

"Here, about five minutes ago."

"Are you serious?" Doug glanced around again, frowned, then waved his arm. "Come on, get in."

"I—I think someone did it on purpose," Gayle stammered, hurrying to climb in beside him.

"Of course they did it on purpose. People don't just accidentally steal a car—" Doug began, but Gayle cut him off.

"No, you don't understand. I think someone planned this. I think someone might be after me."

"After you?" Doug was staring at her as though she were talking some strange foreign language. "What do you mean, someone's after you? Why would someone be after you?"

Gayle shook her head. She held up a hand to silence him. "I think someone followed me here. Doug—I'm really getting scared."

"Hey, calm down. I'm here now—it's gonna be okay—"

"You don't *understand!* You don't know what's been going on—all these horrible things that have happened since we got here—and they keep happening—they just keep *happening!*"

She knew she wasn't making any sense. She could hear her voice rising hysterically, and she could see Doug's face, all worry and concern. As she bit down hard on her lip to keep from babbling, he leaned over and slipped his arms around her shoulders. It was a gesture so natural and sweet and sincere that Gayle didn't even pull away.

"Gayle," he said quietly, "calm down. Tell me what's going on here."

She shook her head fiercely. She hadn't meant to let it slip out, hadn't meant to bring him into this.

"I think someone's after me," she repeated. It was all she could manage at the moment.

"Why do you think that?"

Again she shook her head. She didn't trust herself to speak. She lowered her eyes and took a deep breath.

Doug didn't move. He sat there with his arms around her, waiting for her to pull herself together. At last he murmured, "You know, we've had a ton of car thefts around here lately. Lots of parking lots—even right out of people's driveways. If your car was sitting there with the keys in it . . ."

He left the sentence unfinished. Gayle looked anxiously up into his face. "You mean that? You really think someone just stole my car? That's all it is?"

"What else would it be?"

When she didn't answer, he gently squeezed her shoulders. Then he pulled her closer, resting his chin on top of her head.

"Gayle," he prompted again, "what else would it *be?*"

And she didn't want to tell him, but she did. She told him everything—everything that had happened to them from the minute Stephanie backed into Travis's truck. Doug sat there holding her, not moving, not speaking, just letting her talk. When she finally finished, he brushed his cheek lightly against her hair.

"The Stalker," he mumbled. "God, I was hoping that whole nightmare was over and done with."

"Am I being crazy? I mean, I know the whole thing sounds so ridiculous, but—"

"No," Doug cut her off. "No, you're not crazy. But maybe it's not really as serious as you think. So first we'll report your car to the sheriff. And then . . ." He hesitated, as though thinking carefully before he spoke. "Then . . . we'll go talk to somebody else. Someone who might be able to help."

Gayle sounded hopeful. "Who's that?"

"ClydaMae Wilson."

"What! That psychic in the newspaper?"

"Oh," Doug sounded amused. "So you've heard of her."

"Steph found this article in the paper at Aunt Pat's, but we thought it was a joke. You mean she's real?"

Doug pulled back from her a little. She could see that cute grin spreading slowly over his face.

"Well, she *is* sort of a joke around here. She also happens to be my grandmother."

"You're kidding."

"Would I kid about something like that?" He gave a chuckle and shook his head. "She's the best in the world. A little eccentric . . . but great." He stared at Gayle a long moment, his grin slowly fading. "I don't *want* to think this was anything more than a robbery," he told her. "But I just don't know what to make of everything."

"I don't, either." Gayle frowned. "Do you think people are right to suspect Travis?"

"He always seemed like a decent guy to me. But let's face it—who can you really trust these days? How can you really know a person?" Doug's hands slid from her shoulders, and he took hold of the steering wheel. "One thing's for sure—if your aunt doesn't get back today, I don't think you should stay there by yourself tonight."

"So what should I do? Check into a motel?"

"Come and stay with us."

"I can't do that."

"Why not? My folks would love to have you. And you wouldn't be alone."

"So you *do* suspect Travis."

"I didn't say that. I just want you to be as safe as you can be."

Gayle nodded uncertainly. Was Doug keeping something from her, just so she wouldn't worry? She watched his face as he drove, but it told her nothing.

The sheriff's office was on the other side of town. Doug parked the car by the front door, and the two of them went in together. While Gayle stood by nervously, Doug greeted a big, burly man with a mustache who seemed to be in charge.

"You're Pat Nelson's niece, right?" At Gayle's nod, the man held out a beefy hand. "Sheriff Hodges. So how is Pat these days? Heard she went over to Evanston for the auctions."

"Yes. She's supposed to come home today."

"Well," the sheriff mused, "you've just had yourself one hell of a time, haven't you? First your friend, now your car—"

"You . . . heard about Stephanie?"

"There's not too much in this town I don't hear

131

about," he informed her—rather smugly, Gayle thought. "Doc Maxwell called me last night." His eyes narrowed as he stared at her. "You staying alone over at your aunt's?"

"Yes. Well, not alone, exactly. Travis is there."

"Hmmm." Sheriff Hodges kept watching her. Feeling uncomfortable beneath his scrutiny, Gayle shifted from one foot to the other and fixed her gaze on an empty desk near the door. She waited for him to question her about the garbage dump, but instead of bringing it up, he turned to the desk and began gathering forms from a bottom drawer.

"Lots of cars been disappearing around here lately," he said. "I sure hope you didn't go off and leave your keys in the car. Stupid thing to do. Then acting surprised when someone steals it."

Gayle nodded miserably.

"But we'll catch whoever's doing it. We usually do."

Right, Gayle thought to herself, *just like you caught the Stalker.*

"And what'd you stop out there for anyhow?" the sheriff muttered. "There's nothing out that way—why'd you leave your car?"

Gayle gave Doug a perplexed look. Doug spoke up hurriedly.

"She thought she saw a dog," he said. "She thought it was hurt, so she stopped, but then she couldn't find it."

"Best not to stop for dogs around here," the sheriff told her. "Never know when they might have rabies."

Gayle nodded again and gave him information

about her car, still expecting at any minute to be questioned about the arm in the garbage dump. When the sheriff still didn't bring it up, she wondered if Travis had asked him not to, thinking it might upset her too much to talk about it anymore.

And then another thought struck her.

"Did . . . uh . . . you talk to Travis this morning?" she asked him carefully.

This time the sheriff stopped. He threw her a sharp look—and definitely not a pleasant one.

"Travis? Talk to me? Well, let me tell you, young lady, I haven't seen or heard from Travis Mc-Graw." His eyes narrowed in an ugly sneer. "Travis and I don't exactly have much to say to each other. Or should I say—*he* doesn't have much to say to *me.*"

Gayle's mouth fell open; she felt the surprise showing on her face. So he didn't even know about the arm—Travis hadn't told him! *He lied to me— he said he told the sheriff, that the sheriff didn't find anything in the garbage dump—but the sheriff never even **looked**—Travis never told him **any-thing**—*

Vaguely Gayle felt someone squeeze her shoulder. She looked up into Doug's blue eyes . . . saw Doug caution her with a slight shake of his head. With an effort she struggled to regain her composure.

"Why?" the sheriff asked, suddenly interested. *"Should* he have said something to me?"

"No," Gayle shook her head. "No. I just wondered. I was worried about my aunt, that's all. I was . . . afraid something might have happened to her—an accident, maybe. I asked Travis to check, just to see if any wrecks had been reported. But . . . but she's only at those auctions. That's all it was. I'm glad he didn't bother you with it."

"Well, Pat's usually off galavanting somewhere," the sheriff grumbled. "And she tends to lose track of time. And I can tell you, I sure don't like that arrangement over at her place. She's asking for trouble keeping Travis McGraw around. But, hell, you can't tell Pat anything she doesn't want to hear."

"No," Gayle agreed, "you sure can't."

"You two go on now. We'll let you know, soon as we find out something about your car."

"Thanks a lot."

She felt Doug's hand on her shoulder, nudging her outside, but the minute they were back on the sidewalk and out of earshot, she whirled around in alarm.

"Travis didn't tell them about that arm!" she burst out. "He told me he did, but he *didn't!*"

"Wait—wait." Doug held up both hands, trying to quiet her. "I know what you're probably thinking, but—"

"Well, what else *could* I think! He probably went back there this morning and moved it himself! He needed to destroy the evidence, and he didn't want anyone else to know about it!"

"I know it seems that way," Doug said hesitantly. "But we can't be sure Travis had anything to do with it. Maybe he told you he'd go to the sheriff, just to calm you down. Or maybe he really *meant* to do it—but then at the last minute he just couldn't bring himself to."

"I don't understand what you're saying."

"Well, think about it. If he told the sheriff what you found, then all their attention would be right back on Travis again. They'd be breathing down his neck so fast—"

"But if he isn't guilty, then what difference does it make?"

"You don't know Sheriff Hodges. And you don't know what they did to Travis." Doug hesitated, drew a deep breath. "He didn't have a life, Gayle. They followed him every step he took. They watched him and bullied him and brought him in for questioning all hours of the day and night. They *looked* for excuses to bring him in. They *invented* excuses to bring him in—"

"But that's harassment!"

"Not around here, it's not. Around here it's just Sheriff Hodges enforcing the law." Doug's tone hardened. "They roughed him up, Gayle. Pretty bad. They made his life pure hell."

Gayle stared at him sadly. "Then why didn't he leave?"

"I asked him that myself one time."

"You did? What'd he say?"

Doug's look was grim. "He said he'd never give them the satisfaction."

"Oh, God." Gayle looked down, her heart sinking to the pit of her stomach. "Oh, God, Doug . . . I don't know what to think."

For a moment there was silence. Doug took hold of her arm again.

"Come on," he said, steering her back to the car. "Let's go see my grandmother."

16

Gayle wasn't prepared for ClydaMae Wilson's house.

Little more than a shack, it nestled lopsidedly beneath a wooded bluff, where the roads couldn't reach it and the neighbors couldn't pry. The road ended a good half mile before they got there, and after leaving the car, she and Doug walked the rest of the way through a cornfield.

"There's no inside bathroom," Doug warned as they trudged through row after row of parched cornstalks. "But she has a microwave, and she has a computer. She's eighty-nine years old and still determined to be a best-selling author. Oh "—he winked at her—"and I guess I should warn you, she has visions. And hears voices."

Gayle laughed at the expression on his face. "Is this a joke? What am I *really* going to see when we get there?"

"No, I swear." Doug crossed his heart and

grinned. "I just didn't want you to get scared when she starts making predictions about the future."

"I'm ready for anything," Gayle promised. She smiled as Doug reached out for her hand. Together they walked on with Doug in the lead, and the problems of Pine Ridge and its Stalker began to seem farther and farther away.

"Okay?" Doug asked as she stumbled over a hole.

Gayle nodded. He'd stopped and moved closer to steady her, and their bodies were touching. His damp T-shirt clung to his chest and stomach. . . . There was a fine sheen of sweat along his forearms. He smelled of summer—of grass and earth and sweltering heat—and as Gayle felt his hands slide down her arms, she looked up into his face.

He was smiling at her. She'd never seen eyes that shade of blue—or hair so softened by sunlight.

"You sure?" Doug persisted. When she nodded again, he laughed softly, leaned down and kissed her forehead. "Good. 'Cause I sure wouldn't want anything to happen to you."

Gayle's eyes widened in surprise. Grinning, Doug turned around and walked on, still holding tight to her hand.

"There it is," he announced at last. "See? And there's Gram, right out there on the porch waiting for us."

"Waiting for us?" Gayle peered off in the distance, where a small figure stood waving at them. "Did you tell her we were coming?"

"Nope. She always just knows."

Gayle loved her at once. A tiny, birdlike woman,

ClydaMae Wilson greeted them with a wide, warm grin just like her grandson's. To Gayle's amusement, the old woman was wearing a pair of overalls, a dirty bib apron, and a sunbonnet—along with a pair of faded red sneakers on her feet.

Gayle didn't want to stare, but she couldn't help it. She felt Doug yank on her hand, then he leaned over to whisper in her ear.

"That sunbonnet belonged to her great-grandmother," he explained, trying to keep a straight face. "It keeps her twenty degrees cooler—at least, that's what she says." As Gayle hid a smile, he added, "There's her garden over there. She does all the work herself. Still bakes bread every Friday, too. And makes her own wine." He gave her a sly wink. "I think that's where the voices come from."

"I heard that," ClydaMae scolded, giving her grandson a big hug. "Not bad enough you never come to see me—now you're makin' fun of me, too!" Just as slyly, she winked at Gayle over Doug's shoulder. "'Bout time you got around to visitin' your ole grandma."

"How you doin', Gram?"

"Finer'n a frog hair split in two. And who's this pretty thing? You finally takin' my advice and fallin' in love?"

"I'm thinking about it," Doug replied. He turned to Gayle and said, "She's a friend, Gram. You know Pat Nelson—"

"Sure do. Comes up here every two weeks and brings me homemade jam."

"This is her niece."

Gayle noticed that Doug didn't say her name,

but when she gave him a questioning look, he merely shook his head at her.

"Mighty pleased to meet you, hon. Just call me Gram—everybody does." The little old woman caught Gayle in another giant hug, then ushered the two of them over to the porch swing. "Might catch a breeze out here—then again, might not. You just sit here, and I'll rustle up somethin' to eat."

Before Gayle could protest, ClydaMae disappeared into the house. Doug settled back in the swing, stretching his long legs out in front of him and resting his arm behind Gayle's shoulders.

"I wish she wouldn't go to any trouble," Gayle said, but Doug shook his head at her.

"Oh, she loves this—let her do it. She gets lonely. I keep promising myself I'll come more often, but you know how it goes." He let out a sigh. "Somehow I get busy, and before you know it, months have passed."

"That's how I feel about Aunt Pat."

"Guilty," Doug concluded, and they both laughed.

Within minutes ClydaMae was back, bearing a huge tray of homemade cookies and lemonade. She pulled up a chair beside them, and for several minutes the three of them chatted about Doug's family, the drought, and how the garden was weathering this horrible summer heat.

"Now," ClydaMae announced suddenly. She perched on the edge of her seat and fixed them with a bright, curious stare. "I know you two didn't come 'cause you was interested in my taters and green beans. What brings you here, Grandson?"

Doug took another sip of lemonade before he spoke. "It's really because of her, Gram," he said, nodding at Gayle. "We think she might be in . . . well . . . some kind of danger."

"She is," ClydaMae retorted without the slightest hesitation. And as Gayle straightened nervously on the swing, the old woman added, "Well, she is, Doug, and that's a fact. Just look at that hair."

Two pairs of eyes turned in Gayle's direction. Without even thinking, she ran one hand nervously through her long red hair and stared back at them.

Doug leaned forward with a frown. "Tell us anything you can, Gram. Some pretty weird things have been happening to her since she got here yesterday. I don't understand what's going on— but I do know this. I don't want her getting hurt."

ClydaMae pursed her lips and narrowed her eyes. She took a good long look at Gayle.

"Right smart of you," she said earnestly. "Since this girl's gonna end up bein' an important part of your life."

This time Doug looked startled. He glanced at Gayle, and then that easy grin spread over his face.

"I know you mean well, Gram," he scolded, "but we don't have time for matchmaking. This is serious."

"Damn right it's serious." ClydaMae's smile faded and disappeared. "Let me think on it a second."

She leaned back and closed her eyes. Gayle could hear her humming to herself, and then she began to rock, very gently, side to side. Gayle felt Doug's hand on her arm. As she shot him a puzzled glance, he only held a finger to his lips and shook his head for silence.

Minutes crept by. Hummingbirds flitted among the flowers by the porch. Sparrows chirped from the apple trees in the yard, and from somewhere in the distance a woodpecker hammered persistently. Again Gayle looked over at Doug, relieved when he gave her a reassuring smile.

"I've said it before . . . I'll say it now." ClydaMae's eyes were still closed. Her voice was thin and calm, and she was speaking a lot more slowly now . . . almost trancelike, Gayle thought.

"The Stalker's comin'," ClydaMae mumbled. "Comin' soon. Real soon."

Watching her and hearing the words, Gayle suddenly felt chilled—chilled to the bone, even though it had to be a hundred degrees out here on the porch. She felt Doug's hand close over hers, but she couldn't take her eyes from ClydaMae's face.

"Another girl with red hair," ClydaMae went on. "Name starts . . ." She frowned . . . hesitated. . . . "Name starts . . . with . . . with a . . . lemme see, now. With a *G.*"

A cry caught in Gayle's throat. Doug shook his head at her warningly. ClydaMae rocked some more, cocked her head to one side, and drew a deep breath before going on.

"She'll think he's helpin' her, but he won't be. He wants to kill her, just like he's killed all them others. He's tall, this Stalker. Tall . . . clever. Oh, he's real sure of himself. And he's good with sharp things—got a way with knives and such like that. Someone she thinks she can trust. Only she can't."

Gayle's heart seemed to freeze within her. She

felt Doug take hold of her arm. ClydaMae's eyes fluttered open, and she shook her head, as though coming out of a deep, deep sleep.

"That's all I'm gettin'." The old woman shook her head. "Sorry, Doug."

"It's okay, Gram. You've told us a lot." As his grandmother continued staring at them, his arm tightened around Gayle's shoulders. "Gram . . . this is Gayle."

ClydaMae didn't even look surprised. She merely nodded, saying nothing at all.

"But these visions you have—" Gayle began. She stopped and cleared her throat, forcing back sudden tears. She couldn't think, and her heart ached, and her head was beginning to pound. "If you have these visions," she went on slowly, "then why can't you see who the Stalker is? Why can't you see his face?"

"I've told you everything I'm seein', hon." ClydaMae leaned toward her, sounding truly sorry. "It ain't always clear. Most times it's downright cloudy—more like feelin's 'stead of pictures. You understand what I mean? Like I have this sense of him bein' tall. Strong, too, and not thinkin' he'll ever be found out. But I couldn't paint a picture of his face."

"Why haven't you told the sheriff?" Gayle asked. "So they could try to warn people—"

ClydaMae snorted in disgust. "Bill Hodges's the biggest fool that ever lived! You think he'd listen to me? Why, as far as he's concerned, these are just the rantin's and ravin's of a crazy old woman! I'm the last person on earth he'd ever listen to!"

She shook her head, then reached toward the swing, taking Gayle's hand in one of her own.

"He won't listen, hon, so I'm sayin' this now. I don't know when the Stalker might make his move again . . . or how . . . but he *will*. I was right, what I said before—he's just been bidin' his time, waitin' for his next redheaded girl." She gazed deep into Gayle's eyes. Her voice sounded tired and sad. "Poor child"—ClydaMae sighed—"I'm afraid that's you."

17

"I'm sorry," Doug said as he and Gayle drove back toward the house. "I know what you must be thinking—"

"How can you possibly know what I'm thinking?" Gayle replied. Her eyes were fixed on the window, and the world spun past in a blur of tears. "Have you ever been told you're going to die?"

"She didn't say that, and you're not going to die," Doug said firmly, laying one hand over hers. "I'm not going to let you."

"Oh, I forgot." Gayle threw him a sarcastic glance. "When God sent his angels off on their rounds this morning, I forgot one of them would be fishing down at the pond, assigned especially to me."

A smile played at the corners of Doug's mouth. "You don't believe in a lot of things, do you?"

"I don't know. I don't know what to believe anymore."

"Then let's be honest with each other. Yes, I

think a lot of scary things have happened, and yes, I think you might be in danger. I also think you shouldn't stay at the house alone or say anything about any of this to Travis."

"There you go again. Do you suspect him or not?"

"I just don't want to take any chances. As a matter of fact, maybe you should cancel this whole vacation and go back home."

"In what? I don't even have a car!" Gayle's voice rose in frustration. "And anyway, I couldn't do that. I can't leave Stephanie. And I'm worried sick about Aunt Pat."

"Well, I'm worried about *you.* Though I do feel hopeful about one thing."

"What's that?"

"Didn't you hear what Gram said? She said you were going to be an important part of my life."

"What does that mean? That you're going to find my body?"

Doug let her remark go by. He thought a moment before adding, "She also said, 'He *wants* to kill her.' "

"So?"

"In her vision she didn't actually *see* him going through with it. Didn't actually *see* another girl being . . . well . . . you know."

Gayle's voice trembled. "Wonderful. That certainly makes me feel better."

"I only mean—"

"Oh, God, Doug, I *know* what you mean!" Gayle burst out. "What am I going to do? It could be *anyone!* Travis or—or—I don't know—anyone— it could even be *you,* for all I know!"

Was it her imagination or did his hands clench hard on the steering wheel for just the briefest moment? As Gayle continued staring at him, his blue eyes narrowed, and his laugh sounded forced.

"Me?" Doug echoed. "Why'd you say that?"

"Because . . . I don't know why I said it. Because I just said it, that's all."

"If it were me, don't you think Gram would've recognized me in her vision?" His tone bordered on anger now, and Gayle turned her attention back to the window.

"Why do you want to help me?" she murmured. "Why do you even want to get mixed up in any of this?"

Doug shook his head. "I've got my reasons."

She didn't feel like talking anymore. Beside her, Doug fell into a sullen silence. It seemed to take forever to get back to the house.

"Her car's not here," Gayle said as soon as they pulled into the drive. "Travis said Aunt Pat would be here, but she's not."

She got out of the car and slammed the door. Doug leaned out his window as she started toward the front porch.

"Gayle, come on. Please stay at our house tonight."

"No."

She stopped and looked back at him. His eyes pleaded with her, and for one wild second she actually thought of running straight back to his car, straight back into his arms, straight back to that warm, safe feeling he'd given her, their bodies pressed together in the cornfield. . . .

"No," she said again, more firmly this time. "I

know you mean well, but I can't right now. If Aunt Pat doesn't get home pretty soon, I . . ."

Her voice trailed off. What *would* she do? Travis didn't seem the least bit worried about her aunt being away, and neither did the sheriff. *But something's wrong, something's so wrong. Aunt Pat should be here by now, and Stephanie's gone, too—*

"I'm coming by later to check on you," Doug said.

Gayle snapped back to the present. Had he been talking to her all that time? If he had, she'd missed everything he'd said. . . .

"You hear me, Gayle?" Doug persisted. "I'm coming by later. Will you come home with me then? Will you at least think about it?"

She felt herself nod. "Maybe," she promised. She watched as he pulled away . . . watched the reluctant wave he gave her. Then she went into the house.

Travis was on the back porch, tinkering with the air conditioner again. He barely acknowledged her as she walked into the kitchen.

"You've been gone," was all he said.

Gayle sat down in a chair. "I . . . went for a drive."

"With Doug Wilson?"

"Well . . . see . . . he just gave me a ride home. My car got stolen."

"Where?"

Gayle thought quickly, but kept her voice casual. "I went into this store. Then I came back out, and my car was gone."

"What store?"

"The . . . grocery store."

"And Doug just happened to come by." When Gayle didn't answer, Travis shrugged. "How convenient."

She had a sick feeling he didn't believe her. Even though he didn't actually say so, even though he just kept on working.

"Your aunt called while you were gone," he told her, and Gayle's heart gave a leap.

"She did? When?"

"About half an hour ago. She wanted to talk to you, but I didn't know where you were. She said she can't get home tonight—she had car trouble. And they probably won't get it fixed today, so she might not make it back till tomorrow night."

Gayle felt herself nodding . . . felt her skin going cold all over. . . .

"Tomorrow . . . night?" she mumbled.

"Yeah. She's worried about you—wanted to make sure you're okay."

His dark eyes flicked to her face, then down again. As Gayle followed the movement, she suddenly realized he was clutching an ice pick in his hand, working it deftly back and forth, trying to pry some bits of metal apart.

"I told her not to worry," Travis said quietly. "I told her I'd take good care of you."

18

The afternoon crept by.

Gayle wandered restlessly from room to room, throwing open windows, trying to find one cool spot, one cool breeze. She tried to read but couldn't absorb the words—she tried watching TV but couldn't seem to concentrate. Hours passed. From time to time she could hear Travis swearing and throwing down his tools. The house was suffocating and much too still. Her whole body felt like a wet rag.

She'd almost forgotten about Mark. With all that had happened, their brief conversation at the hospital that morning had completely slipped her mind. By the time she remembered he was coming by, it was nearly six, so she took a shower and changed into fresh clothes.

Why am I doing this anyway? Gayle peered at her reflection in the mirror and made a face at herself. There was something about Mark Gentry she really didn't like, and the prospect of spending even a little time with him wasn't something she was looking forward to. Still . . . she *was* curious about his views on the Pine Ridge Stalker. And knowing that his own sister had disappeared made her feel a certain sympathy for him. How would it be, she wondered sadly, if someone you were close to simply vanished into thin air?

Like Aunt Pat . . .

"Stop that," Gayle said aloud, and this time she glowered at her reflection. "Aunt Pat's fine. Everything has a perfectly reasonable explanation, and she'll be home again tomorrow."

She wished she was more convincing. After a last critical look at herself, she went downstairs only to find the back porch deserted.

"Travis!" she called. "Where are you?"

His project was still scattered in pieces across the floor. Opening the screen door, Gayle stared off across the yard, but there wasn't a sign of him anywhere. Deciding he must have quit for the day, Gayle went into the living room to wait for Mark. Seven o'clock came and went. Seven-thirty. Quarter till eight . . .

Gayle didn't know whether to feel angry or foolish. Why had she even believed him anyway? Guys with attitudes—like Mark Gentry—didn't usually keep their word or take girls seriously. *He probably just wanted to see if I'd give in and say yes. . . .*

She thought she heard a sound from the driveway. *Oh, great, and I suppose he'll have some really lame excuse for being so late and expect me to believe that, too.* Growing more irritated by the second, Gayle got up and went out to the front porch. When she didn't see a car, she decided to check along the side of the house. Just as she reached the backyard and peered off behind the house, she thought she saw someone going into the barn.

Travis? Gayle frowned and shaded her eyes from the sun. Probably shadows, she told herself, nothing more. *Just shadows . . .*

She started to go back, then spun around again. *I must be hearing things—I could swear someone just called me. . . .*

Of course she was hearing things, she told herself sternly. Nothing moved anywhere; the air hung dusty and hot and silent. Yet even as she stood there staring, she heard it again. A soft, urgent cry—*"Gayle!"*

"Travis?"

It had to be him—who else could it be? Anxiously Gayle turned and scanned the front yard, the drive, the hill that sloped down to the road. Nothing moved—the whole place was deserted. She glanced up at the windows of the house, at the roofline and chimney, but the house stared back at her, empty and tired.

And then she heard it again.

"Gayle!"

A pleading cry. Like someone in trouble . . . someone in pain . . .

"Travis!" Gayle shouted. He must be hurt, she realized, he must have hurt himself somehow and needed her help. So she really *had* seen someone going into the barn, and that someone must have been him—

Gayle started to run. "I hear you, Travis! I'm coming!" She reached the door and fumbled with the latch. "Travis?" she called. "Travis, are you in there?"

Funny . . . why doesn't he answer me?

She stopped and listened. No sound came from inside the barn. She inched the door open and stood there awhile, frowning. Maybe he couldn't hear her. Or maybe he'd hurt himself so badly, he'd lost consciousness. *Or maybe he's just trying to play a joke on me. . . .*

She stayed where she was, weighing the possibilities. Travis was always so serious—he just didn't seem like the type who'd play a joke on her—and especially not one like this. . . .

"Travis, if you don't say something right now, I'm leaving. Do you hear me?"

There was no answer.

Gayle shifted from one foot to the other. The barn door creaked open another few inches. She felt a stifling wave of heat and dust and grain, those stale, earthy smells of horses and old leather and birds nesting in rafters. The light from the doorway angled in across the packed earth floor, and dust hung in the air, a thick brown-gold haze.

"Come on, Travis, please answer me," Gayle said softly.

She heard mice skittering through straw. She heard doves cooing from the shadows.

Slowly she started down the left side of the barn. She remembered all too clearly her last visit here—those noises in the loft, those sprinkles of hay floating down to the floor. Nervously she looked up there now. There were too many shadows in this barn . . . too many deep, dark places where things could hide. . . .

"Travis? Travis, are you in here?"

She wished she'd brought a flashlight. Even now, with those murky beams of light angling around her, she wished she'd brought something to help her see more clearly.

She stopped . . . listened . . . moved cautiously forward. She could see the billowy mounds of hay off to her right. . . .

The quick, dark movement of a shadow . . .

Gayle froze.

She drew her breath in sharply.

She turned and squinted through the gloom, staring at the haystack. The air was deathly quiet, yet her heartbeat echoed like a drum in her ears.

I must have imagined it. . . . It's nothing. . . . It's nothing at all—

And then she saw it again.

And this time she was sure—it *was* a shadow—a shadow moving close to the ground, swift and silent, like thick black liquid. . . .

Gayle let out her breath. She forced a laugh from her tight throat and slowly unclenched her hands from her sides.

Of course. *A cat.* Just like the other times she and Stephanie had thought they'd seen something. Only one of the farm cats, and here she was ready to get hysterical over it.

"Okay, you stupid cat, I'm on to you this time. Here, kitty. Come on, kitty. . . ."

Something meowed from the corner. Soft and faint, like a kitten's meow . . . a tiny, helpless whimper.

"What is it, kitty? Are you hurt?"

Gayle heard a rustling in the hay. *So that's where you are, you dumb cat.* Confidently she moved forward.

And then it came again. Louder this time. Only not in the haystack as she'd thought . . . but off somewhere toward her left.

Gayle stopped, confused. "Kitty? You'd better stay still, or I'll never find you."

Something groaned behind her. As Gayle whirled in alarm, she saw the barn door swinging shut. It slammed with a thud, and everything went pitch black.

"Travis!" Gayle cried. "Is that you? Come on, this isn't funny!"

She wanted to believe he was playing a joke on her—wanted *desperately* to believe that's all it was. ClydaMae's prophecy echoed mercilessly through her brain, and Gayle clutched both sides of her head, trying to block out the grisly images she saw there. *No, no, it's a joke, that's all it is, please, please, that's all it is—*

Forcing herself to stay calm, Gayle stumbled back to the door and tried the latch. To her shock, it wouldn't budge. She tried it again, and then started pounding with her fists.

"Travis! Let me out of here!"

Just a joke . . . just a joke . . . don't panic. . . . And what an idiot she'd been, falling for it so easily! Gayle was furious with herself.

"Damn you, Travis, let me *out!* Help! Somebody help me!"

She quit pounding and leaned back against the

door. Her ears strained fearfully through the silence. Was she alone in here? She couldn't hear a sound, only the sickening pulse of her own terror. She took deep breaths and tried to think. *Don't panic, don't panic.* She knew there were several other doors in here—one very close, in fact—but when she felt her way along the wall and tried to open it, she found that it, too, was locked.

"No," she whispered, "please . . ."

The other door was at the rear of the barn, she knew, but it was so horribly dark in here, and the thought of groping her way that far, trying to find a way out, terrified her.

Her eyes lifted to the shadows above her head. Of course. The loft. She could climb the ladder up into the loft and then yell for help from the outside opening. *See?* she scolded herself. *No need to panic. Just find the stupid ladder and climb.*

Slowly she started forward.

Just a joke—if it wasn't a joke, something would have happened by now, you would have heard something, would have seen something. . . .

Oh, God, get me out of here. She was so scared. Maybe she hadn't really heard a voice calling at all—maybe it had been something else, some other kind of noise, and maybe the door had blown shut and stuck, and maybe Travis didn't have anything to do with this at all, and when he couldn't find her, he'd start looking for her and get her out of here. . . .

But there isn't any wind. The door couldn't have blown shut—it couldn't have closed all by itself—or locked by itself. . . .

She'd reached the haystack now. She started feeling in the general direction of the ladder. *Just climb up, one rung at a time. It's easy. You can do it.*

She reached out, groping the air with trembling hands. No ladder. She stumbled, arms flailing in the darkness, grabbing only air where she was positive there'd been a ladder before.

She stopped, sweat pouring from her brow. It was so hot in here, so quiet, and yet so *loud,* so loud with those whispers and rustlings, those faint scurryings through the straw, the buzz of flies, the restless flutter of wings high, high above her. . . .

The birds flew up with a whir.

Just like the birds last night—just like the birds on the windowsill before that brick came crashing down—

Gayle froze. She staggered a little and flattened her back against a wall.

"Who's there?" she whispered, and then, as panic rose up and engulfed her—*"Who's there!"*

A laugh? Had someone laughed? A low, thick laugh deep in someone's throat?

"Who's—" She choked, and immediately slid down the wall to the floor. Someone *was* in here with her—she was *sure* of it—*sure of it!*—someone hiding in the shadows, someone coming after her—*stalking* her—*Oh, God—stalking me!!!*

She tried to scream. She opened her mouth and heard silence surging through her head. *No . . . please . . . no . . .*

What was she going to do? Where could she go? She couldn't see anything—anything at all—yet she knew without a doubt that someone could see *her,* that someone *had* seen her from the very beginning. . . .

Without even thinking she threw herself down on the hay, diving into it, burrowing down, trying to hide. The prickly needles scratched at her skin and tangled into her hair. *Oh, God, help me!*

She couldn't breathe. Hay and dust and unbearable heat packed down around her, suffocating her. She tried to turn her head, tried to find some air, but her nose was closing up, her lungs were closing up, and she was gasping . . . gasping. . . .

Something grabbed her ankle.

Something grabbed her ankle and began to pull, and Gayle felt herself sliding helplessly from the haystack. In a split second the hand moved up her leg—a strong hand, a cruel hand—and it pulled even harder, so that she screamed in pain and tried to kick.

Fighting and twisting, she clawed her fingers deeper through the hay, searching desperately for something to hold on to.

Something slammed into her back. From some distant realm of consciousness she realized someone was kneeling on her, a knee digging hard into her spine. Her leg was free now, but before she could even move, the hand clamped mercilessly around her neck.

Gayle's head snapped backward. She felt her long hair wrapping tight around her neck, cutting into her throat, squeezing . . . squeezing . . .

Again she tried to scream, but everything was going black now . . . everything fading to silence. . . .

Except for the voice.

Except for that low, thick voice whispering so tenderly in her ear . . .

"What took you so long, my love? I've been waiting for you."

19

Gayle wasn't sure how it happened.

One second she knew she was dying—the next second her face fell forward into the hay.

It seemed an eternity that she lay there.

Her throat felt bruised and sore, but the pressure around her neck was gone. Her scalp ached where her hair had been pulled. Her voice felt raw from screaming, and her body was soaked with sweat. She was terrified to move. Somehow she managed to turn her head, and then she lay there, taking in deep gulps of air, trying not to pass out.

She shivered violently. Dazed and confused, she began to realize that she could actually make out some of her surroundings now. As she finally lifted her head, she saw the barn door standing open.

A chill gripped her from head to toe. Was he still here? Waiting just outside, hoping she'd make a run for it?

Quickly Gayle lowered her head. She couldn't get up, couldn't stop shaking. And when a pair of arms suddenly grabbed her from behind, she went straight into hysterics.

"Gayle! Stop it, Gayle! It's me!"

Through a blur of absolute terror, Gayle saw a face she thought she recognized—heard a voice she thought she knew. Still, she scrambled back out of his reach and began to cry.

"Someone was in here!" she said, sobbing. "Someone tried to kill me!"

Mark Gentry looked down at her in total bewilderment. "Kill you? What are you talking about?"

"The Stalker! He tried to strangle me!" Gayle could hardly talk, she was crying so hard. "You must have seen him! He was just here!"

"I didn't see anyone," Mark said uneasily. "I heard someone screaming, and I ran in, but—"

"That's impossible! You *couldn't* have come in here without seeing him! He was here, I'm telling you! Right *here!*"

She was growing more panicky by the second. She could see Mark, standing there staring, shaking his head, and a fierce, hot anger exploded inside her.

"Don't say you didn't see him—you *had* to have seen him! What are you saying—that I *dreamed* it? That I *imagined* the whole thing? Look at my neck if you don't believe me—he had my hair wrapped around my neck—"

"Jesus, Gayle—calm down—"

"Don't tell me what to do! You weren't here, you weren't fighting for your life—"

"Okay, okay, I believe you—"

"And don't humor me! Don't you understand I was almost killed just now!"

She stumbled shakily to her feet. Mark reached out to grab her arm.

"Look, I don't know what you're talking about," he said, "but just stop crying, okay? Whatever happened, it's over now. You're safe."

"But that's just it!" she cried. "I'm *not* safe! Don't you understand—I'm not safe as long as he's out there!"

"What the hell are you talking about!" Mark demanded. "All this stuff about the Stalker—"

"And why did *you* show up just now? Just at this exact minute—"

"I thought we had a date!" Now Mark was sounding angry. "But hey, if you want to cancel, that's fine with me."

"You're the one who's late!" Gayle could hear herself ranting, totally out of control. She knew she wasn't making any sense, but she couldn't stop the words from coming. "If you hadn't been late, none of this would have happened! In fact, maybe *you're* the Stalker! Maybe the sheriff should start keeping an eye on *you!*"

It was a horrible thing to say, and she regretted it the second it was out. Mark's look changed from shock to anger, and he swore under his breath. Jerking out of his grasp, Gayle pushed past him, but he grabbed her arm again and tried to pull her back. Without thinking, she took a swing at him, and as Mark sidestepped her aim, she lost her balance and toppled over into the haystack.

Mark did the worst thing he could have done. He laughed.

Furious, Gayle kicked out with her foot and caught him in the shin, and the next instant he was down on the hay beside her, trying to hold her thrashing arms.

"Right, Gayle, I'm the Stalker," he said, and he was still laughing, but it was a different laugh now—a cold, harsh laugh without any trace of humor. "I'm the Stalker," he said again, "and if I wanted to kill you, I could do it so easily, because there's nobody around, and no one would ever know."

"Get away from me!" Gayle cried, but Mark angled himself across her, pinning her with his body. "I mean it, Mark—get off!"

"That was a hell of a thing to say to me." His teeth were clenched, and his voice trembled. "Now calm down, and stop fighting before you hurt yourself."

His face was just inches above her own. She saw his expression—the mixture of pain and anger—and then suddenly his lips were on hers, hard and demanding, and though she struggled beneath him, he pressed her down into the hay.

Gayle slipped her arms around his neck, responding to his kiss with a passion she'd never felt before. She felt his hands moving slowly down her sides. . . . She felt them circle behind her back and hold her even closer against him.

All the fear and tension seemed to burst inside her. Suddenly, more than anything else, she wanted to hold on to someone, to stay with him forever, to know that she wasn't going to die—

The kiss ended.

Mark's lips lingered a moment longer on hers, then she felt him roll away.

They were facing each other now, lying side by

side in the haystack. He seemed in no hurry at all to get up; he simply stared at her, his gaze traveling slowly and deliberately over her body as he'd done the first time they met. He reached out and touched her cheek.

Then, suddenly, Mark's eyes went wide.

He flung out his arm, and before Gayle could react, he gave her a shove that sent her sprawling back against the wall.

She heard the thing falling before she actually saw it.

Heard the swift slice through the air and the muffled puncture as it stabbed into the haystack.

"My God . . ." Mark mumbled.

But Gayle couldn't even speak.

All she could do was stare at the pitchfork.

It was standing straight up, its deadly prongs embedded deep in the hay . . .

Right in the spot where they'd been lying.

20

"You okay?" Mark demanded.

Gayle felt his hand on her shoulder, and somehow she managed a nod.

"I—I think so—"

"Dammit, what's going on around here?"

"No, Mark—wait!"

Gayle got up shakily as Mark jumped to his feet. She could see some swelling lines of blood along his arm where the pitchfork had scraped him.

"Mark, you're hurt!"

"Where's the damn ladder?"

"I don't know—I couldn't find it, either—"

"There it is—over behind that post."

"No, Mark—please—"

But before she could stop him, he had dragged the ladder beneath the loft opening and was climbing up.

"Don't go up there, Mark! Please don't go up there!"

"Stay here. It's okay."

She saw him disappear into the opening above, and she held her breath, expecting to hear cries at any second and the awful sounds of a scuffle.

But everything was quiet . . . deathly quiet.

"Mark?" she whispered. "Mark, are you okay?"

No answer. Not even a rustle of hay.

"Mark!" she cried again. "Mark, are you all right? Answer me or I'm coming up there!"

Growing more frightened by the second, Gayle put her hands on the sides of the ladder. "Mark, I mean it, I'm coming up. Do you hear me?"

Gayle stood there, her mind racing. What should she do—take a chance and really go up there? Run outside for help? And where was Travis? Hadn't he heard all the commotion—why wasn't he coming to see what was wrong?

"Mark?" she called again. "Mark, please, you're scaring me!"

To her relief she saw his head appear in the opening. "I'm coming down," he said. "There's nobody up here, Gayle. Or if there was, he's gone by now."

Relieved, she held the ladder as he climbed down again. When he touched bottom, he turned and glared at the pitchfork.

"That wasn't an accident," he muttered, and Gayle nodded, trying hard not to cry.

"*Now* do you believe me?" she asked him.

Mark took her hand and started walking toward the door. His normally cocky expression was utterly furious.

"Who's the only person around here who has access to this place?" he demanded.

"Travis, I guess, but—"

"You could've been killed," Mark seethed at her. "We *both* could have. What more proof do you need?"

Gayle clammed up, not knowing what to say. Her legs were shaking so badly, she could hardly keep up with him.

"Where are you going?" she asked.

"To the sheriff."

"I'm coming with you."

"Damn right you are. There's no telling where he might be hiding around here."

"But he's *not* here," Gayle realized as they got to Mark's car. Mark stopped and stared at her as she gestured around the driveway. "He's *not* here, Mark. His truck's gone."

And it might have been gone all this time, she thought wildly. *He might not have been here at all, he might not know about any of this—*

She got into Mark's car. She watched as he slammed his foot on the accelerator, and her mind kept spinning, spinning—*Why are you even considering this—you lied once to protect him, you can't ignore the possibility anymore, not when everyone in the whole town thinks he's the guilty one—*

She pressed her hands hard to her temples. She took a deep breath and looked at Mark.

"Please tell me," she said quietly. "Please tell me about your sister."

Mark was quiet for a long while. Then at last he began to talk.

"I never thought she should get mixed up with Travis in the first place. They weren't anything alike—they didn't have anything in common. Hell, the only reason she did it was to hurt Mom."

"You mean . . . she didn't really care about Travis? She was just using him?"

"She thought the whole thing was a joke. She and Mom never got along, and Mom disapproved of most of the guys she went out with. So Nancy liked to run off with Travis every chance she got. It was just a way to flaunt her independence."

Mark's face went dark with anger. His hands tightened on the wheel.

"The only problem was, Travis was crazy about Nancy. *Too* crazy about her. After a while she told me she couldn't stand his possessiveness anymore, and she wanted to break up with him. But every time she'd try, he'd get furious at her. That last night they had a terrible fight. She told him she wanted to go out with other guys, and Travis went ballistic. Said he'd *never* let her go out with another guy."

"So . . . Travis thought she cared about him, too?"

Mark gave a humorless laugh. "Knowing Nancy . . . probably. She could be real convincing when she had ulterior motives. So convincing, I think Travis wanted to marry her."

"And you're sure Nancy didn't feel the same way? You're sure she didn't love him?"

Mark laughed again. "What sort of life would she have had with him? Not exactly job security, if you know what I mean. No, she'd never have married Travis."

Gayle lowered her eyes. She didn't want to, but suddenly she felt sorry for Travis.

"The day after the argument," Mark went on, "Nancy disappeared."

"And you overheard the argument?"

"She'd asked me to take her over to Travis's that night. She was scared he'd make a scene."

"So . . . no one else heard them. Only you."

Mark threw her a sharp glance. "Are you saying I'm lying, Gayle? That I'd make something like this up?"

"No," Gayle said, flustered. "No, of course not."

"Well, I wouldn't make up something like that—she was my sister, for God's sake. And Travis knew *every* girl who disappeared."

Gayle hesitated. "I didn't know that. Was he . . . serious about all of them?"

"I don't know about his private life. All I know is, people saw him talking to every girl at some time or another before they disappeared."

"But it's a small town. Everyone knows everyone—that's not unusual, right?"

Mark bristled. "Why are you sticking up for him? What's it gonna take before you see the truth?"

"I'm sorry, Mark—I'm not sticking up for him. And I'm really sorry about your sister."

Gayle lapsed into troubled silence. She felt sick and shaky, and she couldn't forget what had happened in the barn. When they finally got to the sheriff's office, the woman at the front desk greeted them indifferently, while people bustled in every direction around the room.

"Go on home now, Mark. Sheriff's too busy for your complaints against Travis."

"Well, tell him this time it's something he can't ignore," Mark returned coldly. "I want him to talk with Gayle—right now."

"He can't right now. Don't you see all the fuss going on?"

"About what?"

The woman leaned forward conspiratorially. "Stalker at work again."

Gayle felt her blood run cold.

"Stalker?" Mark's eyes narrowed. He shifted from one foot to the other; he squeezed Gayle's hand. "What happened?"

"You know I can't give out that information—"

"Come on, Jean, you know I won't say anything." Mark flashed that smile, and Jean smiled back, leaning even closer.

"Well, here it is. Girl over in Evanston. Long red hair. Folks found her room empty this morning—think she must have disappeared sometime last night. Everyone's hysterical, whole town in a panic. You know. The usual."

Mark glanced at Gayle. *See?* his look said. *I told you so.*

"You might know her, Mark," the woman went on. "She just started with the ambulance crew there in town. Glenda? Glenda Eastman?"

Gayle's blood ran cold. *"Name starts with a G . . ." ClydaMae had said. G . . .*

"No," Gayle mumbled. "Oh, no . . ."

"Gayle?"

And Mark was looking at her, and the woman was looking at her, and she was trying to pull away, backing toward the door—

"I have—have to leave," Gayle stammered, "have to."

She turned and stumbled outside. She got out to

the sidewalk and felt Mark's arms go around her, guiding her over to a bench in front of the building.

"Sit down, Gayle. What's wrong?"

"It should've been me," she kept mumbling over and over again. "It was *supposed* to be me."

"What are you talking about? What was? You're not making any sense—"

"Supposed to be me . . ." Gayle's eyes went wide. "ClydaMae said so—"

"ClydaMae Wilson!" Mark exclaimed, making no attempt to hide his disgust. "You been talking to that stupid Doug Wilson? Jesus, Gayle, everyone in town knows his grandmother's as looney as they come! What'd she say to you? No wonder you're so spooked!"

"But don't you see?" Gayle grabbed Mark's arms, her fingers digging into his skin. "Don't you see—ClydaMae was right! It wasn't *Gayle*, though, it was *Glenda*—"

"ClydaMae's insane, Gayle—forget ClydaMae. I'm more concerned about that pitchfork Travis rigged up to kill you with!"

"But how do you know it was rigged? Maybe he left it there by mistake—maybe he was coming back to finish working in the barn—maybe it was just an accident—"

"It came down right where you and I were—"

"No." Gayle shook her head, her grip tightening on his arms. "It could have just fallen—"

"Could have, but *didn't*. What is it gonna take to convince you that Travis is a *killer?*"

"I don't know! Why did *you* show up when you did? How did *you* know where I was?"

Mark stopped, his mouth open. "I told you. I drove up, and I heard you screaming."

"All that way? You heard me screaming all that way?"

"Well, for Christ's sake, Gayle, you were screaming your head off!"

"But the barn was closed up!"

"Okay, so I was walking out by the house—when I knocked and you didn't answer, I thought you might be outside somewhere! And then I heard someone screaming!"

He started to say more, checked himself, and bit down on his lip. Gayle looked down as he pried her fingers from his arms.

"Listen to me, Gayle," he said earnestly, leaning down into her face. "Don't go back to that house tonight. Stay with me."

She heard herself laugh. She saw the puzzled look on Mark's face, and she heard herself laugh again.

"I'm the most popular girl in town," Gayle mumbled. "For all the wrong reasons."

"What's that supposed to mean?" he asked.

"Nothing." She shook her head. "Take me home."

"Take you home? You act like *I'm* the bad guy here!"

"Take me home, Mark. *Now*. Please."

Mark scowled and stepped back. "Fine. Fine, Gayle. Just get in the car."

And *this is a nightmare,* she thought, *a nightmare, the worst nightmare I've ever had in my life—* and she kept thinking it the whole time Mark was driving her back to the house. *A nightmare! And as soon as I'm locked inside and Mark's gone, I'm going to call Doug and have him come and get me, so I can stay at his house till I wake up again.*

She didn't wait for Mark to walk her to the door. As soon as the car stopped in the driveway, she jumped out, said a hasty goodbye, and ran inside. She heard the angry rev of Mark's engine as he left. She ran for the phone, then stopped in dismay to see Travis sitting at the kitchen table.

It was almost as though he'd been waiting for her.

"What happened?" he asked, his eyes going over her in one smooth glance. "Where were you?"

Gayle stared at him. "What are you doing here?"

"Waiting for you. It's late. I was worried."

Should she believe him? Gayle felt like screaming. She wanted to pick up the phone, but she didn't want Travis to hear the conversation.

"Where were you this evening?" she finally asked.

"I had to pick up those screens in town."

"Screens?" she repeated stupidly.

"Yeah. I looked for you, but you weren't around."

"No. I was in the barn."

His expression didn't change; his stare didn't waver. *But what did you expect,* Gayle chided herself, *a full-blown confession?*

"What . . . happened?" Travis repeated, his voice grim.

"There was an accident," she heard herself say, and his eyes narrowed . . . went even darker.

"What kind of accident?" he mumbled.

"The pitchfork. It fell. It barely missed me."

"Are you okay?"

Gayle nodded.

"What were you doing in the haystack?" Travis kept on.

"How'd you *know* I was in the haystack?"

And was it only her imagination or had his expression gone slightly mocking?

"It's the only place the pitchfork could have fallen," Travis answered smoothly.

"If it hadn't been for Mark," she said, "I might have been killed."

"Mark?"

Now there was no mistaking it—no mistaking at all the sudden rush of anger over his face.

"What was *he* doing here?" Travis demanded.

"We . . . he just stopped by."

"I see." Travis nodded. His long fingers brushed slowly across his chin, as though he were thinking. "So he saved you, did he?"

"Yes. In fact, he showed up just in the nick of time and—"

"How convenient," Travis broke in. "How very damn convenient."

Gayle tried to control her own anger—her own rage and frustration trembling together in her voice.

"And what's *that* supposed to mean, Travis?"

"Nothing," he said, getting up and heading for the door. "Which is just as much as *you* know about your wonderful Mark Gentry."

21

Without even realizing what she was going to do, Gayle rushed over and grabbed his arm.

"What do you mean?" she demanded.

Travis looked down at her, his stare cold and unflinching. "Just what I said. You don't know anything about him. Not anything at all."

"Then tell me what I *should* know."

"Hey, I'm just a prime suspect in his sister's disappearance." Travis gave a sarcastic shrug. "Why ask me?"

"Because . . ."

Gayle's voice died away. *Because what? Because I don't want to die, because I don't want to be the Stalker's next victim, because Aunt Pat hired you when no one else would, and I don't want to believe you're guilty. . . .*

"You already think I'm guilty," Travis broke into her thoughts. "So what does it matter?"

"It *matters*," Gayle said firmly.

He gazed at her, and she could see a faint

expression in the black depths of his eyes. Derision? Amusement? Whatever it was, he nodded slowly, then sat back down in his chair.

"Mark knew all the girls who disappeared," Travis began. "He'd gone to school with a few of them—even dated them for a while. Another one used to be a volunteer at the hospital—he dated her, too. And one of them used to go out with Doug—till Mark moved in and stole her away from him."

"Wait a minute." Gayle sat down across from Travis and rested her elbows on the table. "Doug Wilson?"

"Yeah, that's right. Anyway, Mark knew them all"—Travis gave a mocking smile—"intimately."

Gayle nodded, only half listening. *Doug Wilson!* But why hadn't Doug mentioned that to her when they'd talked? With an effort she forced herself back to the present.

"You really loved Nancy, didn't you?" she asked quietly.

She'd expected a response—at least some sort of emotion—but Travis didn't react at all. He simply stared at her, and he stared for a long time. He stared until Gayle finally broke his gaze by lowering her own to the tabletop.

"I'm sorry," she mumbled. "I shouldn't . . . I mean . . . it's none of my business."

She forced her eyes up again. And felt a shock of pure sorrow go through her.

He hadn't expected her to look up so soon, she decided. Hadn't expected her to look up and see him, and so he'd relaxed his guard for that one split second, allowing the pain and the loss and the deep, deep suffering to totally engulf the features of his face.

A wrenching ache went through Gayle's heart.

And in just the space of her heartbeat, Travis's jaw hardened once again, and his eyes narrowed and smoldered black as midnight.

"I loved Nancy," he said.

He sounded almost indifferent.

Gayle continued to stare at him in amazement. How could anyone control their emotions so perfectly, so smoothly, leaving no trace at all of human feeling? *Like an actor,* she thought, *turning emotions off and on as easily as a faucet.*

"I loved her," Travis mumbled again. "A lot more than Mark did."

A shiver worked slowly up Gayle's spine.

"What do you mean?" she asked softly. "What do you mean by that?"

"I mean Mark hated her. She was their father's favorite, and she stood to inherit more in the will. She and Mark never got along. He was always putting her down and making fun of her, telling her she couldn't do things, couldn't succeed. They fought all the time. He had a million and one reasons why Nancy shouldn't stay with me—I wasn't good enough for her, she'd never have a future with me. What did he know about us, anyway?" Travis's jaw clenched. "If he'd minded his own business, maybe things would have turned out different."

Gayle sat there in stunned surprise. "Do you . . . do you think he could have—"

"Killed her?" Travis finished. "I think Mark

176

would do anything to keep someone else from being happy."

Gayle's mind was racing. She didn't know what to believe—whom to trust. She started as Travis pushed his chair back from the table to stand up. She got to her own feet and began talking again before he could leave.

"You didn't tell the sheriff," she said quickly. "You didn't tell him what Steph and I found at the garbage dump."

Travis faced her squarely. "No, I didn't tell him."

"Why not?"

"Because he'd have slapped me in jail, and I'm sick of all the trouble. But I did go out to the dump myself, and there wasn't anything there."

"There *was* something there!"

"Like that hair hanging in your tree?"

Gayle's voice shook angrily. "You *told* me you were going to tell the sheriff, Travis, and I believed you."

"I lied," Travis said. "And you shouldn't trust people you don't know."

He started out the door. A hard knot of fear began to twist deep in Gayle's stomach.

"I'll be back later," Travis added casually. "I'm driving over to Evanston to get your aunt."

"She called?"

"While you were gone."

Gayle stared at him. That shiver was back again, creeping like ice up the length of her spine.

"How come Aunt Pat only calls when you're here, and I'm not?" she murmured, but Travis didn't seem to hear the question.

"She doesn't want to wait around for her car to be fixed," he went on. "She wants me to pick her up."

"Can I go with you?"

"No," he said. *A little too quickly,* Gayle thought. They both jumped as the phone rang. Travis looked at her, and she hurried to answer it.

"Maybe it's Aunt Pat," she said hopefully.

But it wasn't Aunt Pat—it was another voice she recognized at once.

"Gayle, it's Mark," he said solemnly. "I'm at the hospital—I think you should come down here right away."

"Why? What's happened?"

"Your friend looks a lot worse to me. I don't know what's wrong with her—hasn't anyone called?"

"No, but I just got home and—"

"Get down here right away. I need to talk to you."

"What are you doing there? I thought your shift was over."

"They called me to work tonight. One of the other guys couldn't make it in."

Gayle nodded, her voice tight. "I'll see if Travis can bring me."

She put her hand over the phone. "Something's wrong with Stephanie—can you take me to the hospital?"

"Who's that?"

"Mark."

"Mark? Why's *he* calling you?"

"I don't know. Can you take me?"

"Why isn't the nurse calling you?"

"I don't know! Can you take me or not?"

Travis narrowed his eyes. He nodded.

"Mark, I'll be right there," Gayle said, but the line was dead.

Mark had already hung up.

22

"You want me to come in with you?" Travis asked as Gayle got out of the truck.

"No, that's okay. I'd rather you went for Aunt Pat."

Travis hesitated, his eyes going over the front of the building. "Maybe I should wait."

"No, really. I'll be okay. Just go bring her home."

"Yes, ma'am." Travis touched his fingertips to his forehead in a mocking gesture. "I'll just wait till you get inside, please, ma'am, if that's all right with you."

Gayle didn't have time to be angry—she was too concerned about Stephanie. But when she got off the elevator on Stephanie's floor, a nurse stopped her before she could even reach Stephanie's room.

"Sorry, miss, visiting hours are over."

"It's important," Gayle told her. "I won't stay but a minute."

The nurse glanced up at the wall clock. "Well . . ."

"It's *important,*" Gayle said again, more firmly this time.

"Only a minute then," the nurse relented.

Gayle nodded a thank you and hurried down the hall. She turned into Stephanie's room and then froze on the threshold.

The room was empty.

One bed hadn't been slept in at all; the other had messy covers that looked as if they'd been thrown back in a hurry.

"No . . ." Gayle murmured.

She raced back to the nurse's station, leaning breathlessly over the counter.

"Stephanie Borders," she said as two nurses looked up at her in surprise. "My friend— Stephanie—she was in that room—where is she?"

"Stephanie Borders . . . Borders . . ." The older of the two glanced warily at her companion, then down at a chart on the desk. "Stephanie Borders." She nodded. "They moved her to intensive care."

"Intensive care!" Gayle exclaimed. "But why? When did this happen?"

"Are you family?" the younger nurse said primly. "I'm afraid only family is allowed—"

"I'm her friend, and I'm the only family she's got right now!" Gayle snapped. "So you better tell me what's going on!"

The nurse drew herself up and took a step back. "Well, there's no need to get all—"

"When did you take her?" Gayle demanded.

The older one moved forward, her tone soothing. "About half an hour ago. You're the friend who brought her to the hospital, right? Pat Nelson's niece?"

"What floor?" Gayle asked. And as the younger nurse started to interrupt, her voice grew higher. "What floor!"

"Third floor." The younger nurse glared at her. "But you can't go up there—they won't let you see her, and I'll just have to call—"

Gayle didn't stop to hear the rest. She ran for the elevator and pushed the button, feeling like her heart was going to explode.

Intensive care! Why hadn't anyone told her! What could possibly have happened! *Oh, Steph, you were supposed to be getting better—I just saw you this afternoon, and you were supposed to be getting better!* Gayle hit her fists against the elevator doors, trying to hold back her panic. *Don't get upset—it won't do Steph any good if you get upset.* She wished she'd asked Travis to stay with her. She wished there was someone—anyone—she could call!

Mark.

In her shock she'd forgotten about Mark. After all, Mark was the one who'd called her in the first place, and Mark was here somewhere in the hospital. She knew what she'd do now—she'd have him paged. She'd have him paged just as soon as she got to intensive care and made sure Stephanie was all right. . . .

Where was the stupid elevator? What was taking it so long? Gayle stepped back, fidgeting, then stopped with a frown. *Strange* . . .

She whirled around, peering down the corridor. She could have sworn she'd seen something from the corner of her eye just then . . . a figure standing at the very end of the hallway. She stepped back a little and squinted. If someone really *had* been there, the hall was empty now.

The elevator doors opened, and she got on. She pushed the button for the third floor and watched the number light up on the panel in front of her. When the doors opened again, she got off, then stood there uncertainly, reading the signs posted on the walls.

A sudden noise startled her. Turning around, Gayle saw the empty area in front of the elevators, nothing more. *Quit being so jumpy, you're scaring yourself!* She began walking and noticed the door to the stairs, tucked inconspicuously into a corner. The door wasn't shut all the way. In fact, Gayle realized uncomfortably, that noise she'd just heard had sounded a lot like a door swishing open . . . clicking shut . . .

Again she stopped. She could feel goose bumps crawling up her arms. Where was everyone, anyway? This hospital was as lively as a funeral home. With growing unease, Gayle hurried the rest of the way, turning down the east corridor until she finally reached a pair of wide, swinging doors marked ICU. There was a large desk just inside the doors, complete with all sorts of screens and monitors, and one solitary nurse looked up as Gayle burst in.

"Hi, there," the nurse greeted her softly. "Can I help you?"

"I want to see my friend," Gayle said. "Please— I've got to see her!"

"Your friend?" the nurse looked baffled.

"Stephanie Borders. She's not in her room, and the nurse told me she was supposed to come here."

The nurse gave her a kind smile, but was slowly shaking her head.

"Well . . . isn't that the oddest thing. The only patient we have right now is Mr. Phelps. And just between you and me, I don't think we'll have him much longer."

"But . . ." Gayle felt so cold, so strained. It was a struggle just to get the words out. "But what about my friend?"

The nurse leaned forward and patted her hand. "Who was it that told you to come here?"

Gayle's lips moved, but no sound came out. She heard the doors move behind her and another nurse walked in.

"Hey, Betty," the nurse greeted the other at the desk. "You got a new patient here, by any chance?"

"Actually, Fran, I don't," Betty answered. "And I'm beginning to wonder about that."

"Well, I just got a call from Virginia down on two. Said someone was asking about a patient on her wing and wanted to know if she found us okay."

The nurse called Betty nodded at Gayle. "That must be you?"

"Yes. So where's my friend?"

Betty looked sympathetic. "Honey, I'm sorry, but I sure don't know anything about your friend."

"But that's impossible," Gayle murmured. "I mean . . . she's supposed to be *here,* and she's not in her room. So . . . so . . . she has to be somewhere!"

Fran shot Betty a concerned look. "Virginia said

an orderly came for that patient almost an hour ago."

"An orderly did?" Betty frowned. "Who was it? Danny?"

"I don't think Danny came in tonight," the other replied. "I think Mark took over his shift."

The two nurses exchanged troubled looks.

"Well, let me just see about this," Betty said, reaching for the phone in front of her. "I'll get ahold of somebody—see if maybe they took her somewhere else for tests."

Gayle's heart was creeping up into her throat. She could feel her whole body going rigid.

"Why don't you sit down?" Fran said, laying a comforting hand on Gayle's shoulders. "Just wait here a minute, and see what Betty finds out."

"No—" Gayle backed up. *Travis—maybe he didn't leave—maybe he's still outside—* "I mean, yes. I mean, I've got to go now, but I'll be back in just a minute."

Betty was already dialing, but she gave Gayle a warm smile. "Don't worry. I'm sure we'll find your friend by then."

Gayle nodded, swallowed the lump in her throat. She'd almost reached the doors when she remembered something.

"Can you page Mark Gentry, please?" she asked the nurses.

"You know Mark?" Betty smiled again, and Fran added, "What girl doesn't?" and they both laughed.

"Please. It's really important—*please,*" Gayle insisted. "And can you tell him Gayle needs to talk to him—right away!"

Betty nodded. "Sure we will. Mark shouldn't be too hard to find."

Gayle raced to the elevators, her heart pounding. It was like being in some sort of terrible dream— the empty corridors, the eerie quiet—the running and running and getting nowhere at all. *Oh, Steph, where are you!* She couldn't believe this was happening. How could anyone lose a patient in the hospital!

She prayed Travis would still be there. Even though she'd told him to go, even though she'd been so insistent about it. She flew out the front door of the hospital and stopped at the end of the walkway, staring frantically around the parking lot.

His truck was gone.

No—no!

Maybe he'd just moved it, Gayle tried to tell herself, maybe he hadn't really gone, maybe he'd just parked it in another place, and if she looked hard enough and wished hard enough, the battered old pickup would magically appear. Yet even as she stood there, eyes desperately searching the lot, Gayle knew she had to face the truth.

Travis had really gone. Just like she'd told him to.

The lobby—maybe he's waiting in the lobby!

She went back inside. She walked quickly through the lobby, and then past the gift shop— *closed*—and the pharmacy—*closed*—and the coffee shop—*closed. What kind of a hospital is this anyway?* she wondered. *Doesn't anyone in this town ever get sick?*

But of course people got sick, she realized as she saw the huge clock on the wall. People got sick all the time, but visiting hours had ended long ago. It was after eleven, and Pine Ridge Hospital had settled down for the night.

Maybe that nurse was right, Gayle told herself as she hurried back to the elevators—maybe they'd taken Stephanie somewhere for tests. If Stephanie really *was* getting worse, like Mark had said, then it made perfect sense to run tests on her before she went to intensive care . . . right?

Gayle pressed her hands to her head, trying to calm the throbbing at her temples. Maybe there'd been some sort of mess-up in communications, she told herself. Maybe the nurses had just gotten their messages mixed up, and everything was really all right. Maybe Stephanie had gone to the bathroom—maybe she'd wandered down the hall to the TV room—*maybe she was in some other hallway taking a walk, and she wasn't worse at all, maybe she made a miraculous recovery, and I didn't think to go look for her*—

Gayle stumbled and put a hand out to the wall. She was so tired, so worried, she wasn't even watching where she was going. The elevators were just ahead of her now, and she stopped. Off to her right the hallway turned a corner, and as she lifted her head, she thought she saw an abrupt movement, as though someone had started around the corner, then pulled back again out of sight.

Gayle stared, her pulse quickening.

She heard the ding of the elevator . . . heard the doors slide open.

Shaking her head, she got on the elevator and leaned against the wall next to the buttons. She pushed 3 and wearily closed her eyes. The elevator dinged again and slowed to a stop at the second floor. As Gayle opened her eyes, the doors slid back, but nobody got on.

Gayle waited. The doors remained open, and from somewhere down the corridors she could hear the droning voice of the intercom—"Paging Mark Gentry—Mark Gentry—please report to ICU immediately. . . ."

"Thank God," Gayle mumbled. Maybe now someone would know what was going on around here. She stabbed impatiently at the third-floor button. The doors shuddered and began to close.

Without warning, an arm thrust itself inside. As Gayle gasped, she saw the doors jerk, then reluctantly open again. A tall figure was standing there, dressed in a green surgical gown with a surgical cap and mask. Gayle let out a sigh of relief.

"Sorry," the doctor mumbled.

"No problem," Gayle assured him. "You scared me, is all."

"Sorry," he mumbled again.

His head was lowered, but he gave her a polite nod, then stepped to the back, angling himself into the corner behind her.

The elevator rushed up. The doors split wide, and Gayle took one step forward.

"Good night," she said, glancing back at the doctor.

He nodded his head. He seemed preoccupied with his own deep thoughts.

Probably lost a patient, Gayle concluded sadly. And she started out the doors.

She only vaguely heard the movement behind her.

The gauze clamped onto her like a wet skin, clinging to her nose and mouth, the sickly sweet fragrance surging through her head.

Her arms thrashed out. Her fingers clawed frantically.

She saw the doors closing . . . closing . . .

Leaving her alone in the dark.

23

Gayle was lost in her old, familiar nightmare.

Locked inside a coffin . . . trying to scratch her way out . . .

And *no*, she heard someone thinking, *no, I'm still only dreaming, only dreaming, it's not real, and any second now I'm going to wake up, and everything will be all right. . . .*

But in this horrible, realistic nightmare of hers, she *couldn't* wake up, and the coffin lid was *right there*, right above her, and she was lifting her hands, scratching on it, *pounding* on it, but still, no matter how hard she tried, she couldn't get it to open. *I'm buried*, the thought told her, the thought someone was thinking—*Is it me? Is it me thinking that thought? Because I'm buried and this isn't a dream, my God, this isn't a dream at all, this is real*—

Gayle started screaming.

She could hear them, echoing inside her head, muffled and terrified, surrounding her in a dark, close space, and *oh, God help me, I'm buried alive—*

The screams stopped.

Gayle's eyes were open, and her face was wet with tears. She was shivering uncontrollably and freezing cold. *Cold?*

Her mind remembered how hot it had been that day—how terribly hot it had been in the cornfield when someone had held her, when someone had cared about her—*someone in a dream?*

But I'm buried, the thought reminded her. *Buried alive, buried deep, and the ground is always cold, cold even in summer. . . .*

She wasn't screaming anymore. She was very, very quiet, and her heart was choking with terror. She reeked of that sweet, sickly smell, and her mind was swaying, going in and out, full of strange thoughts and pictures that she couldn't control. Then suddenly she heard a sound . . . a dull rumbling sound . . . and from some faraway place she seemed to realize that she was moving.

She gasped as fresh air flowed over her face. She struggled to see, but there was only darkness.

"So you're awake," a voice whispered. It was a soft voice, a whispery voice, a voice that could belong to anyone at all, Gayle thought dully. For a split second she felt as if she should *know* that strange, soft voice—but in the next second it was nothing more than her dream. . . .

"I was hoping you'd wake up soon," the voice slipped back to her, only it seemed much closer now. Close to her head . . . close to her ear. "Let's play a game," the voice said. "A special game. Just for you."

Gayle's heart clutched deep in her chest. And *I do know that voice,* the thought nagged at her—*I know that voice, I've heard that voice before. . . .*

"A game," the voice said again. "Ready? First question, Gayle. Try to guess where you are."

Gayle wondered if her eyes were really open. They *felt* as if they were open, but it was still so dark, and everything was blurry and whirled with shadows. She tried to lift her head, but it was much too heavy. After several starts she finally managed to turn her head to the side, and she fixed her eyes on the murky darkness. She saw a faint light glowing in the distance. She saw a gleaming reflection of tile and stainless steel; she had the unpleasant sensation of cold, stark cleanliness and strong, sterile smells. . . .

"Where am I?" she mumbled. "I don't like it here."

"But it's nice here," the voice whispered back to her. "It's nice and safe."

"Where *am* I?" Gayle tried to speak louder, but the words seemed to garble inside her mouth. Her head felt as if it were floating away from her. She wanted to reach out and grab it, but she couldn't move her arms. "Please . . . please . . . what's happening to me . . . ?"

"I told you," the voice soothed her. "You're here. Playing the game. And if you get the answers right, it buys you a little time. A little more time to live. Now. Where do you think you are?"

Gayle's eyes widened slowly. She fixed them on the glowing light. It didn't seem quite so far away from her now . . . not miles away at all . . . only across the room. . . .

A room.

She tried to concentrate. Lying there with her head angled to the side, she tried to focus on her surroundings, tried to feed the images into her fuzzy brain. *Tile floor . . . tile walls . . . stainless-steel tables . . .*

"Time's almost up," the voice warned softly. "And when your time's up, then you die."

"I'm . . . in the hospital," she murmured.

"Not good enough. *Where* in the hospital?"

And somehow she knew then—somehow from that vague, blurry distance the thoughts were coming faster now, speaking louder to her—the painful cold, the close, cramped coffin, the lid she couldn't open, and that rumbling sound, that sound of her body moving backward—*sliding* backward—even though she knew she hadn't been able to move. . . .

"Oh, God," she whispered. "Oh . . . God . . ."

And not a coffin at all, she *knew* that now—not a coffin at all, but a drawer—*a drawer!*—a refrigerated drawer where dead bodies were stored away, dead bodies in the morgue—

"Oh, God, I'm in the morgue. . . ."

The screams exploded in her head, bursting and bursting in a wild agony of silence. And *"I'll give you the ride of your life," Mark had said. "Care to join me?" Mark had said—*

"Good for you, Gayle," the voice sounded pleased. "A little while longer to live. Next question."

And *why can't he hear me screaming?* Gayle wondered crazily. *Why isn't someone coming!* And why was the room swaying around her like an insane kaleidoscope, and why was Mark's voice fading in and out, in and out, like words in a windy tunnel . . . ?

"Please," she mumbled. "Please let me go. Where's Stephanie? What have you done with Stephanie?"

"Question number two," the voice whispered. "Which drawer do you think Stephanie's in?"

Tears rolled helplessly down Gayle's face. Her breath was like ice in her lungs. She willed herself to move, to jump up, to fly at him, to shriek and rip his face to shreds with her hands—but these were all just harmless thoughts, just thoughts floating through her mind and out again, totally useless . . . as useless as dreams.

"Pick a drawer," the voice commanded.

Without warning Gayle felt herself being jerked to her feet, flopping like a rag doll as he held her by the arms and shoulders and dragged her across the floor.

"Stephanie?" he called softly. "Here, Stephanie . . . here Stephanie . . . Gayle's looking for you. . . ."

"No . . . please . . ."

The voice hardened. "Call her. It's the last thing she'll ever hear."

"What have you *done* to her! Stephanie! *Stephanie,* where *are* you!"

Gayle jolted to a stop. She could feel hands—rough cruel hands—holding her up, forcing her around. She could see the shadowy face, all hazy and liquid, the featureless face with its surgical mask and its surgical cap, with its whispery voice, taunting her.

"Stephanie's not my type, you know," the voice

sounded reflective. "Not like you, Gayle. Not with all that pretty red hair."

She felt his hand on top of her head. She felt it stroking her hair, and she gave a violent shudder.

"But she saw me that night at the garbage dump," the voice went on. "And she saw Nancy, too. Well . . . what was *left* of Nancy."

The voice smiled. The fingers combed through Gayle's hair, slowly, lovingly.

"Sometimes," he told her, "people just end up in the wrong place at the wrong time. Like Stephanie. See, Gayle, I *had* to move Nancy—with all those builders and developers coming to your aunt's farm, they were *bound* to find her. All that digging and digging . . . Nancy deserved better than that. A more—shall we say—*proper* burial." The voice grew hard . . . angry, almost. "It was a private affair, Gayle. No one was supposed to be there. Just Nancy and me."

"You . . . you mean, you buried Nancy on Aunt Pat's farm?" Gayle could hardly get the words out.

"Of course. Close to the one who loved her. Just the way it should have been."

A thick taste of bile rose up in Gayle's throat. She swallowed and forced it back down.

"But Stephanie *didn't* see you!" She tried to get the words out, tried to reason with him. "She didn't see you—neither one of us did. There was a flashlight, and it was shining in our eyes. We couldn't see *anything*. So there's no reason to hurt Stephanie. You could let her go."

"Wrong!" the voice declared. "Not part of the game, Gayle. Now, go on. Pick a drawer. Any drawer."

His voice, like his face, was becoming a blur. As he dragged her another few feet, Gayle struggled to keep her balance, but only collapsed against him. She could smell his sweat, the fabric of his clothes, the mixture of soap and antiseptic. . . .

"I'll help you," he said quietly. "Shall I? Gayle chooses drawer number . . . *three!*"

To Gayle's horror, he wrapped her fingers around the handle and began to pull. The drawer trundled outward, and she saw the body bag lying inside.

"No," she begged, "no, please—"

Slowly his hand reached out. . . .

Slowly he unzipped the bag.

Stephanie's face was ghostly white. There were bruised hollows beneath her eyes, and her cheeks were sunken.

"No!" and from that vast, foggy distance Gayle could hear herself crying now, loud sobs echoing in the sterile silence of the room, loud sobs racking her entire body—"No, please, *please* don't do this!"

"Hospitals are wonderful institutions, Gayle," the voice assured her. "So many drugs at one's disposal. *Deadly* drugs, if one knows how to use them."

"Stephanie . . ." Gayle wept, but the hand was back on her shoulder again, pressing her close against him.

"Oh, she's not dead *yet*, Gayle. Just very close to it. I took the IV out of her before it was too late. Now all she needs is one . . . tiny . . . needle stick."

"Please don't kill her," Gayle begged him. *"I'm the one you want, aren't I? I mean, look at her—*

she doesn't know anything about this! Just please let her go—she doesn't even know who you are!"

The voice laughed softly. "That's true, Gayle. That . . . is . . . true. Actually . . . *nobody* knows who I am."

He dropped her.

He let her go, and she crumpled to the floor, trying desperately to sit up again, trying desperately to scoot away from him. She could see his shadowy figure, looming above her. . . . She could hear the soft laugh in his throat.

"But I'm going to let you in on my secret," he murmured. "Because you and I are so close . . . and because it's the very last thing you'll ever see."

Gayle was paralyzed with terror. Gazing up at him, she saw his slow-motion movements as he lifted his arms . . . peeled back his cap . . . slid down his mask . . .

And at first she didn't even recognize him, at first his face was only shadows, like all the other shadows in the room, but then he leaned down, and he smiled at her, and her heart burst within her—

"Dr. Maxwell!" she gasped.

"I told your aunt about those auctions"—he laughed again—"just so she'd be gone when you got there. And I did a little job on her car, too, so she couldn't get home again right away. And *I'm* the one who hung one of my trophies outside your window. I have a lot of pretty trophies like that, Gayle. You're in good company."

His fingers twined into her hair. She could feel him twisting it, gathering it tightly into his fist. Her head began to tilt backward.

"It's been so easy—so easy, right from the very

start. Moving to Pine Ridge and taking over Doc Yates's patients—I just picked out all the pretty redheads and kept them for myself. It wasn't even hard to dispose of them, really. Not with all the poor little towns and backroads and abandoned farms around here. Why, I've hidden bodies where no one could ever find them. Not a trace. Not in a million years."

His tone sounded almost wistful. He lapsed into silence, then made a sound of disgust in his throat.

"That's not to mention incompetent sheriffs. Like Hodges, for instance—what a pathetic excuse for law and order! If he's lucky—and I mean, *very* lucky—he might even find Glenda Eastman, too, someday. In the trunk of your car, at the bottom of the lake up north of here. It would've been you, of course, but someone came by that day and picked you up before I could offer you a ride. I know . . . because I was watching."

He let out a pensive sigh. Gayle felt his breath on the back of her head.

"Travis was a bonus, really. A loner like him—a troublemaker like him—and one of these days I'm going to personally thank him for keeping all that suspicion away from me."

His grip tightened on her hair. She gasped as her head bent even farther back.

"*I* put the poison in the quiche because, you know, Gayle, *you* were the one who was supposed to eat it. Not your poor friend Stephanie."

"Poison . . ."

"But no one will know that, Gayle. No one but you and I. You see, Stephanie's blood work will come back normal, because *I* know how to fix things like that."

He laughed, immensely pleased with himself. Gayle's head tilted another inch.

"But why?" she choked. *"Why!* I don't understand—"

"But that's the whole thing, isn't it? *Nobody* understands! Nobody *ever* understands!"

Dr. Maxwell leaned closer. She could feel his lips moving lightly against her ear . . . could feel his fingertip trailing lightly across her throat.

"She died on that operating table," he mumbled. "She died because some doctor killed her. Because some doctor was so *incompetent* and so *unfeeling!*"

His breath was coming faster now. Gayle shut her eyes as he rambled on, his voice low and calm and strangely detached.

"They cut off her hair," he murmured. "All her beautiful red hair . . . They said she had a good chance of pulling through . . . that the brain tumor might not kill her."

He drew his breath in sharply. His tone went icy cold.

"And it didn't kill her. That doctor killed her. That *doctor* . . . killed her. . . ."

Gayle trembled violently. She could barely speak.

"I'm sorry," she whispered. "Dr. Maxwell . . . I'm so sorry. . . ."

"Don't be."

Her head snapped back. She cried out—felt like her neck was breaking.

"Don't be, Gayle, because, you see, now I can

have any redhead I want. And when your aunt showed me your picture, *you*—out of all the others—*you* looked so much like *her*. Just like the one I lost. . . ."

"But I'm not her," Gayle whispered frantically. "Don't you see? I'm not her!"

Dr. Maxwell didn't seem to hear. "I'm really amazed at how lucky you are, Gayle. There's always someone around to help you, isn't there?"

He went quiet. He seemed to be thinking.

"But this time . . . your luck's run out."

"Don't kill us," Gayle begged. "Please let us go."

"I'm afraid I can't do that," he whispered.

Something glittered in the half-light. Still trapped in the haze of a nightmare, Gayle saw the scalpel poised above her throat, lowering slowly, slowly toward her neck.

"Game's over, Gayle. You lose."

And she was floating . . . falling . . . eyes drifting shut as she slumped in his arms. And *I'm dying,* she thought, *I'm dying and it'll all be over soon.* . . .

But beyond the dying, she was vaguely aware of something else. . . .

Something pounding . . . pounding . . .

Somewhere in the far, far distance something pounding and throbbing, jarring the awful stillness of the room, and as Gayle managed to rouse herself, she heard Dr. Maxwell swearing, she felt his arms clenching mercilessly around her.

And "Hey!" a voice was shouting—but not *this* voice, not this dangerous, breathless voice—but *another* voice, another voice fading in and out beneath that insistent pounding noise—"Open up in there! You got a delivery!"

200

The arms clenched harder. With a whimper of pain Gayle felt a quick slash across her neck, felt the faraway ooze of blood. . . .

"Hey!" *Pound! Pound! Pound!* "Come on, will you?"

Gayle tried to struggle. She tried to hit out, to scream, but she had no strength or voice. As a fresh wave of terror engulfed her, she felt herself being picked up, she heard a drawer opening, she felt herself being flung inside.

"Not a word!" the doctor hissed at her. "Not a word, you understand?"

He held something up in front of her. Blurry and distorted, it swam there, close to her eyes, and it took her a while to recognize what it was.

A syringe.

"This is for your friend," Dr. Maxwell promised. "This is for Stephanie, if you so much as breathe."

24

Gayle had never felt so helpless.

As the drawer rolled into the wall and the darkness surged over her, she fought to keep from passing out. Pitch blackness—cold—the smell of imminent death all around her—she lay there straining to hear what was going on outside her prison.

Oh God, help me—don't let him kill Stephanie!

"Hey, Doc, what took you so long?" The voice was muffled, but loud enough, clear enough that she recognized it.

Mark!

Gayle's heart gave a leap. She tried to lift her head, but a wave of dizziness engulfed her. Had he slashed her throat—was she bleeding to death? She tried to move her arms, tried to feel the cut on her neck. She felt like she was going to throw up—everything was going blurrier. No, no, she couldn't faint—she wouldn't *let* herself faint, not now, *not now!*

Her mind spun in a thousand different directions. Should she take a chance—scream?—beat on the sides of the drawer? *Help so near and yet so far . . .*

"Mark," she pleaded, but she knew he couldn't hear her, she knew she hadn't spoken aloud. If she thought hard enough, would he *know* somehow? Would he *sense* somehow?

We don't want to die. With every ounce of strength, Gayle directed her thoughts outward, toward the only one who could help them. *Please, Mark, please get us out of here!*

"That door must have stuck." Dr. Maxwell's voice, good-natured and casual. "Sorry to keep you waiting."

"Don't apologize to me," Mark returned. "Apologize to Mr. Phelps here."

"Ah, yes, Mr. Phelps. We expected this, didn't we. I'm surprised he hung on as long as he did."

"Well, Doc, sometimes life's just full of surprises, huh?"

She heard the yell.

From where Gayle was lying, she heard the sudden yell of shock—the sounds of feet hitting the floor. Almost immediately the room was filled with crashes and bangings, the tense babble of voices, things hitting walls, breaking and shattering on the floor. She tried to get out, but she couldn't get the drawer open. She called for help, but the noise was deafening, and she knew that nobody could hear her.

Then silence.

Total and complete silence.

Silence so deep and so long, that the fear gripped

her even colder and she lay there, too afraid to move.

"Gayle!"

And drawers being pulled—the roll and thud of drawers being pulled and slammed shut again—and Mark's voice—"Gayle! Gayle, are you in here!"—and another voice joining it, a voice just as urgent—"Gayle? Gayle, answer me!"—Travis's voice—Travis . . .

"Help!" she tried to scream, but her voice was so thin, so muffled. "Help—I'm in here!"

"Jesus Christ!" she heard Travis exclaim. "I found Stephanie!"

"Is she alive?"

"I don't know—I think so—"

"Get help down here!" she heard Mark shout. "It's an emergency—we need help down here!"

And then a faint glimmer of light—Gayle saw a faint glimmer of light growing brighter and brighter, heard the rumbling sound as she slid back into the air, into the room, into Mark's arms—

"Here she is! Gayle, are you okay?"

And both of them holding her, helping her, lifting her to safety, as the room came slowly into focus again and she saw their smiles.

25

"Best barbeque I ever ate," Stephanie declared, wiping a thick glob of sauce from her upper lip. "In fact, I think I'll just have one more rib, if you don't mind."

"If you don't stop eating, you're going to be sick all over again," Gayle teased, but Aunt Pat gave a hearty laugh.

"You'd better have more than that, my dear. Travis fixed enough to feed an army. Doug—ClydaMae—help yourself—there's plenty."

"So what do you think about this handyman of yours, anyway?" Gayle nudged her aunt. "I bet you didn't know he was such a great chef."

"There's a lot about me you don't know," Travis said, glancing at her. For a long moment their eyes held, then he turned back to his cooking.

Mark Gentry got up from the picnic bench and stretched. "But she probably doesn't *want* to know," he threw at Travis. "I mean, why would she even want to know about you, when I'm so much more fascinating?"

Stephanie burst out laughing. "And arrogant," she said. "Don't forget arrogant."

Mark grinned at her. "Yeah, okay. That, too."

"Now tell me what happened again." Stephanie tried to keep a straight face. "Tell me what happened while I was dying."

Gayle moaned. "Not again. They've only told you two hundred times."

"Hey, this is my first whole day out of the hospital, and my first decent meal. Besides, this is *my* party, so you have to be nice to me!"

"Yeah, she *likes* to hear it," Mark returned, deadpan. "She likes to hear the part where I ran in and saved the girls."

"You did," Stephanie egged him on. "*You* did. All by yourself. Of course, Travis had nothing to do with it."

"All Travis did was pretend to be dead," Mark explained. "That's not exactly what I call heroics, just lying there and pretending to be dead."

"Well, it seems to me—and stop me if I'm wrong," Gayle broke in, "that Travis threw the first punch."

Mark hedged. "Well . . . I mean . . . it didn't knock Maxwell out or anything like that. Just that one punch."

"No"—Gayle nodded—"I believe it was his *second* punch that knocked the good doctor out."

Stephanie stared at Mark. Mark gave a huge sigh.

"I shoved," he defended himself. "I did an awful lot of shoving."

"I couldn't have done it without you," Travis spoke up.

As everyone laughed, Aunt Pat leaned forward across the table.

"Well, I'm sure everyone finds this all very exciting, but when I think what might have happened—and there I was, shopping in Evanston the whole time—"

"But you didn't know," Gayle soothed her. "How could you know? And it worked out all right in the end."

To her surprise she felt tears pricking behind her eyelids. Abruptly she stood and walked away, busying herself at the lemonade cooler while the others continued to joke and talk in the background.

All right in the end . . .

And yes, she thought to herself, even for poor Nancy Gentry, things had finally worked out all right in the end. . . .

"You okay?" a voice murmured, and she looked up to see Travis leaning over her, his face softer somehow, as though he knew.

She nodded . . . choked down the lump in her throat. "I was just thinking about Nancy."

"I know." His eyes lowered. "Me, too."

"I'm just so glad Dr. Maxwell confessed. That they could have a proper burial . . ." Her words trailed away. "I'm so sorry, Travis."

For a moment he didn't answer. Then at last he said, "Mark apologized to me. He wanted me to have Nancy's ring."

"He did?"

"I told him to keep it. I figured it'd mean a lot more to him."

"I'm really glad."

"Hey, Gayle!" Stephanie shouted, and Travis moved back again to the grill. "I'm the guest of honor today, remember? Lemonade, if you please!"

"Coming right up!" Gayle saluted and filled a fresh paper cup.

"You're missing all the good details," Stephanie scolded as Gayle sat down beside her.

"Steph"—Gayle sighed—"I was *there!*"

"I know, but it's such a good story. A *happy* ending. Thanks to Mark," Stephanie added. He winked at her, and she winked back.

From the end of the table Doug Wilson shook his head in awe. "Well, it still amazes me how Mark put everything together like he did."

"It amazes Mark, too," Travis replied.

Mark shot a look in Travis's direction, which Travis pointedly ignored. "It just didn't seem right to me," Mark went on, "that Stephanie wasn't hurt that bad, but she kept getting worse." He leaned back, crossing his arms over his chest. "Then when one of the nurses asked me to deliver some stuff to Maxwell's office, that's when I found those phony lab reports on his desk. That's when I called Gayle."

He nodded at Gayle, and she groaned and picked up the story.

"And then Stephanie disappeared," she recited. "And you didn't know where she was."

"Right." Now Mark leaned toward Gayle, his voice low and intense. "I called you from Maxwell's office. When I went out again, he was just coming in, acting like everything was normal—but

I think he must have heard me on the phone. When I went in to check on Stephanie, she wasn't in her room. The nurses said she'd been transferred to ICU, but before I could get up there to check on her, I ran into Dr. Maxwell again. He told me he'd scheduled Stephanie for some emergency tests, that he was really concerned about her condition."

"And you believed him," Gayle murmured.

"I did till I went around to every room and couldn't find her. But I *did* find your earring in the elevator."

"It must have come off when Dr. Maxwell grabbed me. I think I managed to fight him for about two whole seconds."

"Clever girl, though. Leaving a clue behind."

"Trust me, it wasn't planned. I can't believe you even recognized it."

"Hey, I don't forget *anything* about girls I've flirted with."

Gayle smiled sweetly. "Then you must have an infinite memory."

It took several minutes for the laughter to die down again. Doug stretched his lanky frame across the table and helped himself to more potato salad. "So then what happened?"

"After he found the earring, that's when *I* saw him," Travis obligingly continued. "He ran out the front door of the hospital like someone was after him."

"I was trying to find security," Mark scowled. "Those idiots are never around when you really need them." He shrugged. "So I found the next best idiot instead."

Everyone applauded. Travis conceded with a stiff bow.

"So you *did* wait for me," Gayle teased him.

"Yeah," Travis mumbled. "I waited for you."

"But you said his truck wasn't there," Stephanie reminded Gayle. "Isn't that right?"

"I was parked around on the side," Travis admitted. "So I could see the door but—"

"No one could see you," Mark finished. "I believe your plan was to tail us if Gayle and I left together." Mark affected a mock sneer. "At least give me *some* credit—if I was going to sneak off with her, I'd at least have used the back exit."

"Well . . ." Travis thought a moment. "I had a pretty good view of *that* parking lot, too."

Doug grinned and perched on the end of the table. "I have to admit, I'm jealous not being part of the hero team. That was quite a rescue."

"It really was Mark's idea," Travis said generously.

"Actually, the morgue was the last place I thought of." Mark grew pensive. "But it made perfect sense, didn't it? It's way down in the basement—not a place anyone especially likes to visit, and the door's always locked. Except we could hear Maxwell in there talking to someone, but nobody was answering him. And everyone knew old Mr. Phelps probably wouldn't last through the night—I figured Maxwell wouldn't suspect a thing."

ClydaMae's laugh cackled through the air. "Well, I bet Doc's face went white as all get-out when that corpse got up and swung at him!"

As everyone joined in, Aunt Pat slipped an arm around each of the girls, hugging them tightly.

"Well, all I know is, you're safe. And we're here together. And that's what matters."

"And remind me in the future, *never* to go on vacation with you again," Stephanie scolded Gayle.

"What do you mean?" Gayle teased. "You've got everything you wanted—excitement . . . adventure . . . even the guys, hot dates, and passionate summer romances—"

"Did she say she wanted that?" Mark broke in with a sly smile.

"I forgot one thing," Stephanie returned, just as slyly. "I forgot the hero part."

"I'd settle for air-conditioning," Gayle sighed.

"And being an important part of my life?" Doug prompted cheerfully.

Gayle pretended to be in deep thought.

"After I get my air-conditioning," she conceded.

"Well, tell my handyman." Aunt Pat waved an arm in Travis's direction. "He can fix anything. Anything at all."

"Yes . . ." Gayle mused, looking over at Travis.

He glanced back with just a hint of a smile, his black eyes fixed steadily on hers.

"Yes," Gayle said again, "I believe he can."

About the Author

Richie Tankersley Cusick loves to read and write scary books. Richie enjoys writing when it is rainy and gloomy outside, and likes to have a spooky soundtrack playing in the background. She writes at a desk that originally belonged to a funeral director in the 1800s and that she believes is haunted. Halloween is one of her favorite holidays. She and her husband decorate the entire house, which includes having a body laid out in state in the parlor, life-size models of Frankenstein's monster, the figure of Death to keep watch, and scary costumes for Hannah and Meg, their dogs. A neighbor recently told them that a previous owner of the house was feared by all of the neighborhood kids and no one would go to the house on Halloween.

Richie is the author of *Vampire, Fatal Secrets, The Locker, The Mall, Silent Stalker, Help Wanted, The Drifter, Someone at the Door, Summer of Secrets,* and the novelization of *Buffy the Vampire Slayer,* in addition to several adult novels for Pocket Books. She and her husband, Rick, live outside Kansas City, where she is currently at work on her next novel.

Summer
by Katherine Applegate

Three Months. Three Guys.
One Incredible Summer.

June Dreams 51030-4/$3.50

July's Promise 51031-2/$3.50

August Magic 51032-0/$3.99

Spring Break Special Edition
51041-x/$3.99

Sand, Surf, and Secrets
51037-1/$3.99

Rays, Romance, and Rivalry
51039-8/$3.99

 Available from Archway Paperbacks
Published by Pocket Books

Printed in the United States
By Bookmasters